# MALL-O-WEEN MISCHIEF

## AN AT THE MALL HOLIDAY STANDALONE NOVELLA

### SARAH ROBINSON

# CHAPTER ONE

## JAY

"THAT'S A RIDICULOUS COLOR FOR A DOG," Dr. Jekyll Storm said as he cast a long look at his sister. It had been a while since they'd been in the same place for long, but ever since he'd moved back to town, it felt like she was glued to him. "It's neon orange, for God's sake."

"I mean, some dogs *are* orange, Jay," his sister Winter replied, shrugging her shoulders as they walked past Pugs & Kisses, the local pet store and groomer in the Yule Heights Shopping Mall. "Like those little Shiba Inus, some Golden Retrievers, and I bet you can find an orange chihuahua or two."

He shook his head. "No, those are brown. Maybe reddish brown if you want to stretch your imagination, but definitely not like that Pumpkin Spice Labradoodle in the window."

Winter paused in front of the pet storefront and watched the orange-dyed dog that was wearing a pumpkin collar running around in a pen with a visitor petting him—probably considering adopting him. "But he's so cute! Look, I bet he's up for adoption. We could get a dog."

Jay had zero time for his younger sister's theatrical fantasies. It was bad enough that she was basically a carbon copy of their mother—the human who actually thought naming him Jekyll would be a great idea, sparking his decision to go by Jay since quickly learning in grade school that children did not take kindly to anyone slightly outside the societal norm—but he was certainly not going to indulge Winter's impulsiveness on top of all of that. Being the son of the local Wiccan leader and alchemy shop owner was absolutely not considered normal, something his sister embraced, but Jay fought hard against.

"First of all—we? I thought you were staying with me *temporarily* after that entire mess with Summer," Jay reminded her, purposefully throwing in Winter's ex-girlfriend's name as a small dig. She'd completely melted down when that relationship had ended, and now Jay had to literally work in the same mall as her since Summer owned the local tanning salon. He just avoided the east wing of Yule Heights Shopping Mall as much as possible in hopes of not having another awkward encounter. "Now you think we're adopting a dog together? Absolutely not. And, second, I work way too many long hours to be taking care of a dog."

Winter rolled her eyes so loudly he could hear her annoyance. "Sorry we can't all be doctors and stare into people's eyes all day. Some of us are actually out there trying to make a difference, you know."

Now it was Jay's turn to be irritated. "Optometrists do a lot more than just look in people's eyes all day, and being a doctor is the literal definition of making a difference in people's lives. Posting TikTok videos where you transition between masc looks and feminine looks is barely considered clickbait."

"That's not what my one point two million followers would say," Winter snipped back.

Jay had to consciously relax his jaw when he noticed he was gritting his teeth. God, he needed to check in with her therapist sometime soon.

"Are you guys looking to adopt?" A tall woman with short, black hair that was only interrupted by one orange streak across her side part walked out of the front door of the pet store and smiled at them. There was something engaging about her that immediately made his stomach tighten—like he felt the need to defend himself from...feelings? He wasn't sure what. "I see you guys have been looking at Pumpernickel in the window there."

"And it's named Pumpernickel?" Winter practically swooned as she looked back at the dog on the other side of the glass.

"We could not be less interested," Jay informed the woman, trying his best not to notice the way her figure perfectly filled out the graphic T-shirt and dark jeans she was wearing. "It's inhumane to dress up a dog like that and dye its fur. The poor thing looks ridiculous."

The woman's nostrils flared and her hands perked on her rounded hips. "Excuse me? I'll have you know that Pumpernickel *loves* to be groomed and pampered, and we use only the best pet-safe fur dye on the market."

Winter put a hand on Jay's chest and pushed him back slightly. "I am so sorry about my brother. He's new here and has no idea what he's talking about."

"I can talk about dogs, Winter," Jay cut her off, but didn't bother to push back. "If she can't take some constructive feedback, then maybe she shouldn't be dying dogs for Halloween."

"They," the angry human in front of him corrected, and the fire in their eyes was intriguing. Jay's attention perked up as they continued to speak. "My pronouns are they/them. Not she."

Jay blinked once, twice...then shook his head. The person standing in front of him clearly looked like a woman, so he wasn't sure what the hell they were talking about. "Okay, and my pronouns are doctor. So, what game are we playing now?"

Winter smacked him in the chest hard this time. "Oh my God, Jay. You can't just disrespect people's pronouns like that. They just told you they're nonbinary. That's not the same as going to eye doctor school and getting a certificate."

"It's optometry school," he corrected Winter. "And it's not just a certificate."

"I'm sorry for my older brother," his sister continued, refusing to acknowledge him. "He's a boomer in a millennial's body. I'm Winter—do you own Pugs & Kisses?"

"Avery," they introduced themselves with a thin, clearly forced smile. "Yeah, I'm the owner. I opened Pug & Kisses about two years ago. My brother owns the jewelry store down on the west end of the mall—Val Rossi?"

"We love Val." Winter was now using her sugary-people-pleasing voice, and Jay immediately recognized when she was in damage control mode. Though, if he had to guess, it was probably only because Winter wanted to ask Avery out since Winter was always looking for the next great love to completely upend her life.

His sister's emotional rollercoaster love life was way too much of a hassle to keep up with and he liked to steer clear of it entirely.

"Who's Val?" Jay couldn't remember meeting a jewelry store owner, but then again, he'd met a lot of mall shop owners in the last month and it was hard to keep everyone straight. Yule Heights Shopping Mall was constantly bustling, and there was a steady turn over in storefronts, but a few loyals who seemed like they'd been there since the start.

Winter cut her eyes at him. "Mara's husband?"

"Oh, the arcade owner." That woman, he remembered. She'd already cornered him last week to hustle him into joining the Yule Heights Halloween Storefront Contest, and now he had to somehow decorate an optometrist front window for a spooky holiday.

Like that made any sense at all.

"You seem fun," Avery added in a tone that implied the very opposite. Suddenly a light went on in their eyes, and Jay wasn't sure why his skin felt electric the moment he saw it. "Oh God, please tell me *you* are not the one replacing Dr. Juarez?"

"Dr. Juarez sold me his practice when he retired, yes," Jay confirmed. "But I'm changing the name. Eye Caramba doesn't really fit my style."

"Agreed. You and fun definitely don't seem like a match," Avery responded nonchalantly.

His nostrils flared at the jab. "Or maybe Storm Optical Care is just more professional, and I'm an actual professional—something you might want to learn a bit about yourself."

"Stormy eyes? Sounds like a romance novel description." Avery's hands were back on their hips and they seemed to level their gaze at him, as if daring an escalation in conflict.

Winter laughed. "They actually have a point, Jay. Stormy eyes is very romantic."

The irritation was getting thicker in Jay's blood. "It's *not* a romance novel. Our last name is Storm—I'm Dr. Jekyll Storm. It's named after me."

"Jekyll?" Avery's brows lifted so high on their forehead they nearly touched their hairline. "Your first name is Jekyll? You can't be named that *and* also be an asshole. You've got to just pick one."

Winter was laughing harder now. "Okay, now I definitely want to adopt a dog from them."

"Remember you live rent-free under *my* roof," Jay tossed out there, trying hard not to roll his eyes. That wouldn't be very professional, after all.

"Hey, guys! Looks like you've met!" Mara walked up to their little trio at that moment wearing her signature flannel shirt tied around her waist, oversized jeans, and sleeveless shirt that showed off an arm full of tattoos. Her hair was dyed platinum with orange and black streaks in it—clearly she was another person who liked to celebrate the holidays with Halloween only a week away. He could see why Avery and Mara were friends already. "This is great for me—two birds, one stone."

"Hey, Mara." Avery smiled at their sister-in-law. "What's up?"

"The Yule Heights Halloween Storefront Contest is going to have a store crawl for all participants who will then vote at the end on which stop was the best decorated stop," Mara informed them, holding out a clipboard in front of her and scanning over it with a pencil. "And since Eye Caramba is such close proximity-wise to Pugs & Kisses, we're going to group your storefronts together into one stop on the crawl."

"It's Storm Optical Care," Jay corrected Mara. "I'm going to change the sign this week."

Mara looked stricken, her head rearing back as she turned to look up at him given that she was at least a foot shorter than he was. "But it's been Eye Caramba for fifteen years."

He shrugged. "And now it's Storm Optical Care."

Mara shook her head and seemed to push the whole thing away mentally as if that was beyond her scope of focus for the moment. "Okay, whatever. The point is, you two can decide if you want to coordinate to do a joint storefront, or if you'd rather do two separate themes."

"You want me to team up with *him?*" Avery threw out the words like an accusation. "Mara, come on. I've never won this contest and this was going to be my year. I'm not sharing the spotlight with anyone else."

Mara grinned. "I like the optimism, but like I said, you guys decide. If you want to be separate, then I'll make one stop with two voting options. Just let me know before Friday."

With that, she walked away, flipping her Halloween-themed hair over her shoulder.

"I'm not teaming up," Jay immediately filled the gap between them. "Because I'm not doing it at all."

Avery blinked slowly and even Winter looked up at her brother in surprise.

"You're just not going to decorate for Halloween?" Avery seemed confused. "Literally every storefront in the mall does it. It's like, tradition. Holidays are a big deal in Yule Heights."

He shrugged. "Well, they are not a big deal at Storm Optical Care."

"Jay, I could just get a few paper bats and tape them to the front windows," Winter tried to intervene. "It doesn't have to be extensive."

"My store is a professional one, not a gimmick," Jay replied. "No bats. No decorations. Just professional eye care services."

"You really like that word, don't you?" Avery cut their eyes at him before turning away to head back into the pet store. "Soooo professional."

He could hear their last words huffed under their breath, and it took everything in him not to snap back. But then Winter began pushing him to keep walking now, sending apologetic looks back at Avery.

"I'll talk to him. I'm sorry!" she called out.

The moment they were through the front entry of Storm Optical Care, his sister glared at him. "You know, I have a name in this town. I've lived here for a long time, and this place is really special. You're just coming back into town after nearly a decade away, and the first impression you want to make on the town—and, side note, potential customers—is that you don't give a shit?"

Jay rounded the front counter as he considered what his sister was saying. "Would people really think that? Like it would impact customer retention?"

"That was the part you choose to focus on?" Winter shook her head. "Typical."

Jay was thinking about the entire thing now like a marketing ploy. Being a stop on this Halloween mall crawl would bring a lot of potential customers to his front door and introduce them to the new name. "No, no, I mean, you do have a point."

Winter tossed up her hands as she dropped into a

nearby chair. "Whatever gets you there, I guess. But you need to go talk to Avery about it."

Jay glanced toward the store entrance with a pit of dread—and maybe some excitement—in his stomach. Clearly, he hadn't made friends out of his new neighbor, but could they be teammates?

# CHAPTER TWO

## AVERY

"He's insufferable," Avery groaned as they leaned across the front desk next to the cash register at Pugs & Kisses.

"I am really going to miss Dr. Juarez," Lizzy said from where she was standing by a display near the front window of cute greeting cards that all had different animal themes to it. She was busy organizing the cards and stacking new ones they'd just received in earlier that morning. "He was always so funny on Halloween. Remember when he put all those bloody eyeballs in front of his store and the warning tape? I mean, I think that probably lost him some customers, but it was hilarious as hell."

Avery grinned—that was definitely one for the books. "He emailed me last week that he and his wife are all settled in their new house in the Florida Keys. Apparently, it's everything they dreamed retirement would be and more, so you can't really blame him for that."

"Jealous," Lizzy shot back. "Ask him if he has a guest room for visitors."

"Maybe we could send Dr. Jekyll down there and he never come back," Avery commented.

"I still can't believe his name is actually Jekyll." Lizzy laughed, placing the last greeting card on the rack and then turning back to Avery. "I mean, do you think his parents hate him?"

"Who?" Adim, one of the animal caretakers on staff at Pugs & Kisses, walked up to them to catch the tail end of their conversation. "I want the tea!"

"The man who bought out Dr. Juarez's store after he retired." Avery nodded their head in the direction of Eye Caramba—or, Storm Optical Care now, apparently. "His name is Jekyll Storm."

Adim's eyes lit up. "Wait...is he related to Winter Storm?"

Lizzy looked over at Avery with a confused frown. "I follow her on TikTok, but I thought that was like a stage name. Her real name is Winter Storm?"

"Real name," Avery promised her. "She's always hanging around the mall, even though she doesn't work here. That entire family is strange."

"Well, duh," Adim huffed, as if that was the most obvious thing he'd ever heard. "I mean, don't you know who their mom is?"

Both Avery and Lizzy were focused on Adim now. "No. Who is their mom?" Avery asked.

"Calliope Cross," Adim answered. "Remember that whole scandal a few years back surrounding the alchemy store at the end of Main Street? Their mom owned that store before she went to jail."

"Jail?" Avery's brows shot up. "What happened?"

Adim pulled up an article on his phone and handed it over to Avery to read. "According to the article, it was eleven years ago, and I was a kid when it happened so I probably don't have all the details right, but basically, she murdered their father. Or, he went missing and no body was ever found."

"Excuse me?" Lizzy balked as she leaned over Avery's shoulder to read the same article Avery was now skimming.

"I mean, they can't prove that, but Jericho Storm was last seen in that shop. To this day, she still won't tell officials what happened to him or where he went, so they decided she must have killed him. Maybe like a spell or hex, or something. She's a witch, you know. Her own words."

A shiver ran down Avery's back. "Holy shit...do you think this is why he didn't want to decorate for Halloween?"

Lizzy shrugged. "I mean, if he's already worried about being seen as a possible murdering witch's son in this town, then maybe he doesn't want to add to the gossip mill by putting skeletons out—literally."

That was a fair point, and now Avery felt the slightest bit bad for the annoyingly professional eye doctor. His entire back story just sounded traumatic as hell, and also a pretty good reason to be an asshole now. Or, maybe a reason *not* to be an asshole if he didn't want to be grouped in with his family history...but still. That kind of past couldn't possibly breed a happy person, and Avery felt a tinge of sympathy toward the grumpy neighbor next door.

"So, what are you going to do?" Lizzy lifted her eyes to Avery. "Team up with him for the contest, or no?"

The new information from the last few minutes had just upended that entire decision for them. "Well, now I have no idea. I mean, if I pair up with him...does that make it even spookier? Almost like I'm bringing in a ringer."

Adim laughed and shook his head. "Or it's too real-life

creepy even for Halloween, and people skip this stop on the crawl altogether out of fear for their lives."

"I think *that's* a little extreme," Lizzy told Adim. "It's not like *he's* the murderer."

"Technically, they haven't proven his mom is either," Avery reminded them both. "I mean, I wouldn't want to be judged for something Val did, or our parents did. They make their own choices, and so do I."

Still scrolling the article, Lizzy paused and turned the camera screen to point it at Avery. "Wait, is this him?"

At the end of the article was a photograph of Jay and Winter that must have been taken in quite a few years ago as they both looked younger, more innocent than the duo they'd just run into.

Avery nodded. "Yeah. Jekyll. Or Jay. I kind of like Jekyll better though."

"He's hot," Lizzy commented, her eyes widening. "That makes him even more suspect."

"What? How?" Avery furrowed their brows.

"Serial killers are always really hot white guys, at least according to every Netflix documentary I've seen," Lizzy continued.

Adim nodded in agreement. "I mean, hot is subjective, but with a different haircut, young Dahmer could tap this."

Avery grimaced. "Good lord, I need friends who don't spend their free time in the true crime world."

"They called us friends," Adim said, this time looking at Lizzy. "That's at least two steps up from part-time seasonal employees."

"You guys *are* friends," Avery insisted. "Hell, that's how you got the job. You didn't think I hired you for your workmanship, did you?"

Adim laughed at that quip and Lizzy just shook her head. "Boss got jokes now."

"Go talk to him," Lizzy encouraged them. "I bet he is probably really sad and lonely. Especially with the holidays coming up. Go tell him he's welcome in our corner of Yule Heights Shopping Mall!"

"Wow, you're quick to presume innocence." Avery lifted one brow at their friend. "He wasn't exactly a joy to be around earlier."

"Sounds like a classic defense mechanism." Lizzy was currently in her self-help, pop-psychology reads phase and was diagnosing everyone within a ten-mile radius of different psychological disorders. "What he clearly needs is someone to reach out and help him learn to be more open and vulnerable with others since he's probably really closed off."

"Okay, Dr. Phil," Adim added. Clearly even he had reached the end of his rope. "Everyone has baggage. Maybe the guy's just a dick."

"Well, he's a really hot dick." Lizzy shrugged again. "Plus, Dr. Juarez would want us to be welcoming. He wouldn't have sold his practice to someone he didn't think was a stand-up guy."

Avery groaned at the subtle guilt trip. "Ugh. That's true. Dr. Juarez was a true gem. Jekyll might be highly suspect, but if Juarez vouches for him...he can't be the worst."

With that, they flattened their shoulders and took a deep breath. "Okay. I'm going to go talk to him."

Both Adim and Lizzy rooted them on, and Avery walked out the front entrance and took a direct right toward where Eye Caramba—or, now, Storm Optical Care—was located caddy corner to Pugs & Kisses. When they got to the front door, however, it didn't give as they pulled on the handle.

Avery frowned and glanced through the glass; their hands cupped around their eyes to see more clearly. The inside of the store looked dark, and they didn't see anyone so they knocked loudly on the glass instead.

Suddenly, a man's face appeared on the other side of the glass, inches away from theirs.

Avery shrieked and jumped backwards just as Jay opened the front door.

"Christ, why are you screaming?" Jay frowned as he peered out at them. "You act like you just saw a ghost."

"Well, you just popped up like a jack in the box," they countered, huffing defensively. "Or should I say Jekyll-in-the-box?"

He pushed the door open wider, leaning against it as he crossed his arms over his chest. And, good God, did the man have a chest. Not that Avery was focusing on that. But it was hard not to notice that he had pecs only gifted to someone who spent a lot of time chiseling it out at the gym. "Ha. Never heard that joke before."

"Really?" Avery grinned.

Jay continued to stare; his expression dead faced. "No. Of course I have. I did spend twelve years in public school, you know."

They grimaced and nodded. "Yeah, I was wondering how that went for you when you said that was your full name. I can't imagine kids were super nice about it. That, plus the whole thing with your mom..."

"What whole thing with my mom?" His eyes narrowed and his relaxed posture suddenly stiffened. He looked like he was about to run...or fight? They weren't sure which, but it was clear that a button had just been triggered.

"Oh. Uh, I mean, um...it's a small town, you know?" They tried to put on a polite smile without actually making eye contact with the man. "People around here talk."

"Great, so I guess this is your way of coming over to let me know that I should keep my distance, right? Not taint your reputation with the Calliope Cross's son cloud." His arms were somehow even tighter across his chest, like he was hugging himself. Something about the motion seemed less defensive and more...sad.

Avery couldn't help but want to reach out and touch his arm, like a small peace offering. His skin was warm beneath their palm, but steely hard. "That's not what I was going to say at all."

Jay glanced down at their hand on his arm, but he didn't move away. When his eyes returned to theirs, there was something more than fear behind them...something smoldering.

"I was going to ask if you wanted to join forces for the contest," Avery heard themselves saying before they'd even made a decision on that topic yet. "Like a joint theme across both of our stores, you know?"

He frowned, narrowing his eyes just enough to say he clearly didn't trust the nice gesture. "Why?"

"Instead of questioning it, how about you just say thank you and we shake hands like two professionals?" Avery pulled their hand back from Jay's arm and held it out for a shake instead. "Isn't that what professionals would do?"

Something softened in his expression now, and there was almost the tiniest twitch of a smile at the corner of his lips. "That *would* be very professional," he agreed, taking their hand with one firm shake. "All right. A team. Any specific theme you're already thinking of?"

They let go of his hand and shrugged. "I was thinking possessed puppies, but I'm open to collaborating."

"Possessed puppies?" Jay's brows lifted almost to his hair line. "So, you're the scary decorator type, huh?"

"I mean, it *is* Halloween," Avery pointed out. "The spookiest ones always win the contest."

"And terrify children from every asking their parents to adopt a dog from you," he pointed out.

Avery paused. "Okay, I hadn't considered that aspect. Maybe we should go back to the drawing board."

"I'm finishing up here, but why don't I meet you after your shift at the bar on the west end? Alcohol is great at inspiring ideas," Jay commented. "What's that bar called again? Lucky Lepers?"

Avery laughed and shook their head. "The Lucky Leprechaun, you weirdo. But sure, meet you there in an hour?"

He nodded, then stepped back into his store and let the door close between them.

"Okay, I guess that means I'm going now," Avery said, this time mostly to themselves, as they turned and walked back to Pugs & Kisses.

*Thugs & Hisses? Mean Mugs & Disses?* There had to be a theme that would be scary enough to win the contest, but also keep their customer base. At least they had the rest of the evening to brainstorm it out over a couple glasses of booze with a ridiculously handsome eye doctor. Not that Avery was interested in said eye doctor. Definitely not, not even a little.

# CHAPTER THREE

### JAY

THIS WAS DEFINITELY GOING to be a mistake. Jay wanted to tell himself that inviting Avery out to drinks after work had been more of a strategic decision for the contest, but he could have just stood there in the doorway of his store and brainstormed a few ideas with them.

Instead, he'd asked them out for a drink.

Because all good strategic decision making happened over a glass of alcohol.

Jay thumbed the edges of the cocktail napkin in front of him, then took an extra-long sip of the old fashioned he had ordered when he first arrived. He glanced at the time on his cell phone screen again—Avery was late.

"You waiting on someone?" A tall woman with deep red hair came to a stop in front of him on the other side of the bar.

He barely lifted his gaze—not because he didn't want to look at this woman, but because he didn't want to see the way she was looking at him. Pity was a feeling he was all too familiar with from strangers, and it made his insides want to scream.

"I'm fine. They'll be here soon."

The woman behind the bar shrugged, and there was something gentle about the way she spoke. "All right, but if you need anything, I'm Saoirse. Happy to help, even if it just means a listening ear."

She walked away, and Jay stared after her. He wondered what that was like, to be someone who just checked in on strangers. Instead of being the stranger people felt they needed to check in on.

"You look like you're ten steps deep into an existential crisis sitting here," Avery commented as they slid onto the barstool next to him seconds later. "What's wrong?"

"Nothing," he commented, sitting up straighter and leaning forward into the bar. "This is just my usual face."

"Yikes."

He turned to look at them and Avery was smiling wide —they were teasing him. Something about it didn't spark his defenses, and instead he chuckled. Lightly, but still...he laughed.

Progress.

"Can I get you something to drink?" he asked. "I already ordered."

"Yeah, sorry I'm running a bit later than I meant to. We had a cricket outbreak." Avery placed their elbows on the bar top and flagged down Saoirse. "Hey Saoirse, can I get a margarita on the rocks, no salt?"

Saoirse reached across the bar and squeezed Avery's hand. "Anything for you."

"You know her?" Jay asked once Saoirse had walked away to prepare the drink.

"Saoirse?" Avery's brows were scrunched when they turned to look at him. "Everyone knows Saoirse and Nell. They're like the heart and soul of the entire mall."

Jay straightened his mouth and nodded. "Wow. That's high praise. Hold on...did you say cricket outbreak?"

Avery nodded as they picked up his glass and sniffed the old fashioned, then took a quick sip. "I'm just going to try it."

"Thanks for asking first," he commented. "Should I be worried about this cricket thing?"

"Uh, well..." Avery looked like they were trying to skirt a direct answer. "If you happen to find a few stray crickets in your store, that's my bad."

His eyes widened. "A few?"

"We dropped maybe a hundred, but probably no more than that," Avery continued. "My employee, Lizzy, was transferring them from the box they were shipped in to the box we display them in. There's like cardboard paper towel rolls and stuff in there that they cling to so you just transfer it from one to the other."

"I'm guessing something went wrong during the transfer?" He could already feel his skin crawling and found himself checking his surroundings for invading crickets.

Avery grimaced and let out a sigh as Saoirse dropped off the margarita in front of them. "One of the crickets touched Lizzy's hand so she panicked, dropped the whole roll. It's *very* hard to contain crickets once they get loose. I think I got most of them, but...well, you just let me know if you find some."

"I'm sure you'll hear my screaming from next door," he assured them. "I'm not a bug person."

"Really?" Avery prodded his shoulder with a light poke. "Big, muscly guy like you can't handle a cricket?"

"Not *a* cricket. One hundred crickets," he reminded them. "Who buys crickets anyway?"

"People who want to feed their snakes, frogs, mice,

whatever." Avery took another long gulp of their margarita. "We don't just sell pets, but also pets to feed the pets."

Jay tried not to laugh at that comment, but a small chuckle escaped. "That is morbid as hell."

"The circle of life," Avery teased, placing their glass back down on their own cocktail napkin. "But, um...about what I said earlier..."

Jay glanced sideways at Avery, his brow furrowed as he searched his memory. "What did you say?"

Avery crossed one leg over the other and angled their body to face him. "That stuff I heard about your mom. I mean, this really *is* a small town. But I'm not trying to judge you or anything. I hope it didn't come across that way."

He looked away, hiding the conflicting emotions that surged through him in that moment. "I'm sure you meant well."

"But?" Avery pushed.

Jay hadn't planned a follow up to that response, but something about Avery made him want to keep talking. "But, it's just something I'm used to, I guess. My mother's story has been so sensationalized. It's no wonder people follow it."

Even saying that felt like sugarcoating the entire experience, but this wasn't a topic he normally spoke about—to anyone. It wasn't that it was private—more so that it was the opposite of private. It had been so deeply invaded by the public and law enforcement and everyone he had known back then that it felt...violating. But the way Avery was talking to him didn't feel that way. Instead of guarded or cautious like he normally felt, Avery sparked a feeling of sadness, or maybe it was vulnerability, in him that felt both really wonderful and truly terrible.

Strange how emotions can be so painfully comforting all at the same time.

"Yeah, I get that it must have been sensationalized for the public, but those people aren't living it," Avery pointed out, their hand resting on their knee. "I can't imagine what it must be like for you and Winter—"

"We don't need anyone's pity," Jay cut them off before taking another long gulp of his drink. "We're both fine. I mean, well, I'm fine. Winter is a fucking mess half the time."

The vulnerability he'd felt a moment ago crawled back behind his shield and felt closed tight.

Avery grinned at that remark and let out a small chuckle. "Yeah, I've heard that, too. But I wasn't talking about pity."

He wanted to change the topic now. It had been enough. Too much, even. "Great, but we really should be planning our decorations instead of this mindless chit chat."

A flash of something crossed Avery's expression—maybe hurt? But then a shield of their own seemed to go up that Jay was all too familiar with. Guilt set in as he realized he might have triggered that in Avery.

"I mean, it's not mindless," he said, trying to walk it backward. "I just...we should probably start brainstorming."

Avery nodded, all business as they sipped the last of their drink and motioned to Saoirse for another round. "What is your normal go-to Halloween decor?"

"I don't have go-to decor," he replied. "I can't remember the last time I've decorated anything."

"That tracks." Avery laughed lightly as Saoirse placed two fresh drinks in front of them and took their empty glasses away. "We go all out every year for basically every holiday. Last Halloween we did Zombie Dogs and Cats, and the year before that we did Headless Pets."

Jay grimaced. "Christ. You went straight for gruesome."

"Yep. I love it, but now that you've brought it up, I do think it maybe hurt customer acquisition for a bit. Octobers were a bit slower historically over the last two years." Avery tapped a finger to their chin. "So, maybe horror and gore *aren't* the way to go?"

"You're talking to a witch's son, so I think you already know my answer," Jay joked.

Avery's brows lifted with a small grin. "Oh, so you do have a sense of humor under there somewhere."

"What if we did pumpkin and autumn themes," he suggested, deflecting the compliment. He took a long sip of his second drink and tried to calm the swirling feeling in his stomach at that tiny piece of external validation that Avery had just offered him. "That's kid-friendly."

"That's so boring, though." Avery frowned. "There has to be a middle ground somewhere that is family-friendly but still has a little spice to it. Remember, we want to win this contest, and everyone is going to go all out. We need something unique that no one else will think of."

They both sat there silently for a few moments as Jay wracked his brain for some ideas.

"Maybe I should call Winter. This is more her strong suit than mine," Jay admitted. "Although, I have a feeling she'd struggle with the family-friendly aspect of it."

Avery grinned and shook their head. "I'm friends with Summer, her ex-girlfriend. I've...I've heard things. Again, small town."

"The Storms really like to feed the gossip mill, I guess," Jay postured. "All the more reason why I prefer to stay out of it. The rest of my family shares more than enough to keep everyone entertained. Or horrified, depending on how you look at it."

"I'm not horrified," Avery responded. "I think I just feel...well, maybe sad? But not in a pity kind of way. More so in a compassionate way. Does that make sense?"

He tried not to roll his eyes, but he failed. "Sounds like pity."

Avery shook their head. "I know, but it's more like I couldn't imagine my life without my parents and my brother. All of us are really close, and they really make me who I am, but only in the best ways. It sounds like your experience hasn't been that, and I can't imagine what that must be like. I mean, just not knowing what happened to your dad..."

Jay downed the second half of his old fashioned in an attempt to push away the lump already forming in his throat.

"It's just a lot for someone to go through," Avery continued. "I'm sorry you've been through so much."

"Ghosts." Jay placed the now-empty glass down on the bar top. Saoirse cleared it away almost instantly and he indicated that he wanted one more. "We should do ghosts. That can be family friendly. Almost comedic. But, still on trend and a little spooky."

Avery paused at the sudden change in topic. "People *are* very familiar with ghosts."

Something about the way they said that felt like a deeper meaning, as if he was the one haunted by his own ghosts. And maybe he was.

"Ghosts also don't have eyes, right?" he continued, not pausing to allow the vulnerability to sink behind his shields. "And I'm an eye doctor. So, I could do like glasses for ghosts. Ghoulish glasses."

"How do my dogs fit into that theme, though?" Avery asked. "It's a pet store. Dogs don't wear glasses."

An idea struck him and he sat up, turning to face them. "But dogs do help people with glasses sometimes!"

"You want me to do a seeing-eye ghost service dog?" Avery looked skeptical.

He shrugged one shoulder. "I mean, you said it had to be unique. This could be educational, family-friendly, and still a little spooky."

Avery seemed to sit with the idea for a moment, then nodded their head. "Okay, I can kind of get on board. But, if we're going down this route, then it needs to be truly educational and also supportive of that community. We often work with a nonprofit in the next town over that trains service dogs, so what if we used this as a way to help gather donations for them and raise more awareness around their mission? I know they are always looking for volunteers and people to help train the dogs—it's an intensely long and emotional process."

"I love it," Jay agreed. "I don't actually know too much about that training process, so I'd be interested in learning. And the more we can help others learn about it, the better."

Avery slapped their hand on the bar top. "Well, this calls for a celebration round!"

Saoirse was already dropping off the third round of drinks before they'd even asked. "Not that I was eavesdropping," she said. "But I totally love that idea. Let me know if you need any help. Nell is really great at that kind of thing, too. She used to train service dogs before she took in Laura Dern."

"You live with Laura Dern?" Jay's brows lifted, intrigued.

"The snake. Not the actress," Saoirse clarified.

Jay grinned, feeling like he was part of something real and genuine for a moment. It was really nice to feel included and like he was being invited into a community—even if these people were a bit wacky and apparently snake owners. Still, he couldn't remember the last time he'd felt this light, and while this was a forced matchmaking situation because their stores were neighbors, it still felt like more than that.

It felt like acceptance. He wasn't sure he liked it, but the smile on his face seemed to indicate otherwise.

# CHAPTER FOUR

## AVERY

"I'm just surprised you guys agreed to team up," Mara said as she sat on a stool across the kitchen island from where Avery was leaning against the counter.

Avery was fiddling with the fake spider web laid out across Mara's countertop from last year's Halloween decor. Now badly tangled, it had taken nearly twenty minutes to pull the yarn webbing apart. "I mean, he's not as bad as he comes off."

Mara's brows lifted as she sipped a cup of coffee she'd recently brewed. "Don't lie to me in my own kitchen now, Avery."

Avery laughed and shook their head. "I'm not! I think he's a little guarded, you know? Probably doesn't trust people easily. You saw that article about his family."

Mara grimaced. "I knew Winter was a few crayons short of a full box over the spring when she and Summer had that whole falling out on TikTok, but, damn, I never guessed a back story like that."

"Right?" Avery felt a twinge of guilt—was this gossiping? That wasn't the goal, but it felt a bit like that. They tried to remind themself that they were defending Jay, not trying to bash him. "Either way, they've had a rough go of it. It seems like Jay's the one who takes care of Winter and probably took care of their mom before that. He might actually be the sane one of the bunch."

"I mean, that's not exactly a high bar," Mara teased, placing her coffee cup back down on the counter. "What time did he say he was going to be here?"

Avery had confirmed via text with Jay last night that he'd bring his truck by to Mara and Val's house today to pick up the Halloween decorations that they were loaning them. When he'd first told them he had a truck that could fit everything, Avery hadn't known what to do with that information. So far, they'd only seen him in a crisply starched suit and tie, sometimes with a doctor's white coat on top, and sometimes without. The man reeked of his favorite word—professional.

But apparently, professional also drove a pick-up truck. Color them intrigued.

"Ten thirty," Avery confirmed with Mara. "I need Val to help load everything with Jay."

"Val's at the store already. Opened early today," Mara commented. "We can handle it, the three of us. I've got two kids watching Mickey Mouse in the next room who could probably carry a ghost or two by now."

Avery grinned, shaking their head. "Leave my niece and nephew alone."

They'd loved seeing their brother's life flourish over the last few years since he'd met Mara. A happy home, two children, and a house—Val was living the suburban dad dream. Avery wasn't sure that they saw something like that for themself, but they were proud of Val for chasing his dreams and building the life he wanted. Although, to be honest, Avery would give more credit to Mara than Val for that.

Avery's phone lit up on the kitchen counter and they glanced down to see a text from Jay that simply read *here*. He was a man of many words, clearly.

"Jay's outside," Avery informed Mara. "I'll bring out the first box and then show him where the rest are."

"Let me just check on the kids really quickly, then I'll join you," Mara agreed, already heading for the living room where Avery's niece and nephew were watching a PBS children's show.

Avery laid the now-untangled spider web down carefully in the box, folding it out of necessity, but trying their best to keep it from getting tangled up again. Hoisting the entire thing into their arms, they headed out the front door and down the porch steps just as a large blue pick-up truck with giant tires backed up slowly into the driveway. It came to a stop and the front driver side door opened to Jay stepping out of cab.

"Here, let me carry that," he said the moment he noticed them walking toward him.

Avery wasn't about to complain, but they also found words a little bit hard in that moment. Not because the way Jay had dropped down from the front seat of the cab looked like something out of a movie. And definitely not because he was wearing jeans that were perfectly tight on him and a flannel long-sleeved shirt that looked like it might rip over his biceps. Nope, neither of those factored at all into the dry feeling in Avery's throat as they watched him load the box into the rear of his truck.

He turned back to them when he was finished. "Where's the rest of the stuff?"

"Uh." Avery cleared their throat. "Mara's inside."

"Okay..." Jay furrowed his brows, giving Avery the once over like they had a screw loose. "But where are the decorations we're supposed to pick up?"

"Oh, yes. The garage. I'll show you." Avery turned on their heel and headed around the side of the house to the garage where they'd stacked everything up earlier today that they'd sorted out from the basement. They indicated a stack of boxes and storage containers against the side. "Everything against this wall is going in the truck. Mara will be out to help us in a minute. She's just checking on the kids."

Jay surveyed the stack and then shook his head. "No need. I'll get this stuff loaded and then unloaded at the mall."

"I can help," Avery's response sounded defensive, and they weren't sure where that came from. "It's not like it's that heavy."

"I know," Jay replied, this time looking at them with more of a softness. "It's just that I'm going to be shit at the decorating part. That's where I'll really need your help. Carrying boxes is something I can actually do."

"Oh." That made sense, and there was also something deeper behind it. Like he needed to feel like he could do something himself, but also that he was willing to lean on them. "I am very good at decorating, but I might need some help with the tall stuff."

"That, I can also do." Jay grinned and then headed for the boxes, picking up two in one go and heading back toward the pick-up truck.

Despite his claim, Avery still picked up a few loose items here and there and transported them back to the pick-up truck alongside him. By the time Mara came outside, they were already almost done.

"Damn, that was fast," Mara commented, hands on her

hips as she watched them. "Anything you guys need from me?"

Jay shook his head. "No, I'm just going to take these back to the store now."

Avery suddenly remembered that Mara had picked them up earlier so their car wasn't here. "Mara, can I borrow your car to follow him?"

"Just ride with me," Jay cut in, gesturing toward the passenger seat of the cab. "No need to take two cars if we're going to the same place."

Mara lifted her brows and gave Avery a sly grin. "Yeah, Avery. Ride with Jay in his pick-up truck."

Avery narrowed their eyes at Mara for a brief second, then glanced toward Jay. "Okay, but only because it's more environmentally friendly. I mean, I'm sure this truck killed a dozen trees this week alone."

Jay let out a laugh and shook his head. "It's electric, but okay."

*Shit.* He was even eco-conscious under all that professionalism. "Oh. Well, okay then."

When Avery rounded to the passenger side of the truck, however, they came to a dead stop. "Jay, I can't even reach the door handle over here."

He chuckled right behind them, and Avery nearly jumped, not having realized that he had followed them. "Let me help."

Jay reached across their shoulder and pulled at the door handle above their head, swinging open the door which then released a set of steps that came down lower to the ground. Even then though, the bottom step was high off the ground and Avery looked uncertainly at it.

"Why does it have to be so high?" they asked.

"I mean, what else would contain my massive ego," Jay joked, now offering them a hand. "Want a lift?"

They went to take his hand, but he moved it to their side instead and in one quick motion, gripped their hips and lifted them straight up and onto the passenger seat. Avery felt like a rag doll in his arms and the bra-burning feminist inside them hated how much they liked it. But...they really liked it.

Jay closed the door, and Avery quickly fumbled with pulling on their seatbelt. They tried to ignore Mara waving in the rearview window and making obscene gestures with her tongue between her index finger and middle finger. God, they hoped Jay hadn't seen that. And, God, now their mind was wandering to places it definitely should not be.

Without any difficulty, Jay opened the driver's side door and hopped into his seat. He turned on the radio as the car roared to life, and Avery tried not to be impressed by the fact that he was listening to an all eighties and nineties music radio station. Not because that's what they usually listened to as well, but also...completely because of that. Ironic that one of their favorite songs was Billie Jean by Michael Jackson and yet, the entire song was about banging a chick in a club and then refusing to claim paternity of her son.

Nope, nothing problematic about that at all.

"Thanks for the ride," Avery finally said as he pulled out onto the main road and turned in the direction of the mall. "I do have a car, but I tend to avoid driving unless I absolutely have to. This is such a small town, you know."

"I'm finding that out more and more every day," he confirmed.

Avery was reminded of his background. "Yeah...it can

be really good in a lot of situations, but definitely not all of them."

"That is a factual statement," Jay agreed, then glanced sideways at them. "It's obvious you're curious, but I do appreciate the fact that you haven't pushed. Most people want me to give a full interview by now about my mother."

Avery shrugged. "We all have parts of our past that we don't like to dwell on."

Jay regarded them with skepticism. "You? Everything about you screams sugar plums and garden gnomes since birth."

"Gnomes?" Avery laughed and shook their head. "Okay, I do actually have a little gnome fairy garden built into the tree in my front yard, but I don't know how the hell you could tell that just from looking at me."

"It's not a bad thing," he assured them. "It's just the way you carry yourself. Like a sense of ease and safety. Some people—people like me—we don't know what that's like. We're born into hyper-vigilance and we have to be."

They were nearing the mall at this point, and Avery felt a sadness at what he was saying. "Sometimes I forget that. My life hasn't always been perfect, but I have always felt safe and supported by my family and friends."

"I'm glad you had that," Jay commented, and his words didn't sound jealous or bitter. He sounded genuinely happy for them, like he wanted everyone to have that experience even if it hadn't been in the cards for him.

"Just because you've had to be one way, though," Avery continued, their voice softer now. They reached across the cab and placed a gentle hand on Jay's knee as he drove into the mall parking lot. "Doesn't mean you have to be that way forever. It doesn't mean that you can't find people and places who are safe one day."

Jay didn't turn to look at them, but they saw him swallow and look out the window. Finally, he spoke and his voice sounded husky, as if it were close to breaking. "That's nice to think about. Harder to find in real life."

Avery didn't respond right away but waited until he pulled the truck into a parking spot and placed the vehicle in park. They removed their hand from his knee and pulled off their seat belt then twisted their body to look at him. "I know you don't know me very well—and same, vice versa. But, I'm a safe place. If you want me to be."

Jay didn't meet their eyes. "That's what I'm worried about."

With that, he opened his door and jumped out of the truck, leaving Avery sitting there wondering what the hell had just happened. What had he meant by that?

And what did Avery hope he'd meant?

# CHAPTER FIVE

## JAY

"Brother, I love you, but you're playing with fire," Winter said to him as Jay closed the front doors to the store at the end of the day.

It was unusual for Winter to ever be the voice of reason, and yet, here she was.

"Nothing is happening," he assured his sister, trying not to let his gaze drift to the right where Pugs & Kisses was also closing up shop for the day. "We're friends. Friendly. Neighborly, really. Nothing more than that."

"You're lucky I'm here to help you guys decorate tonight," Winter mused, tapping a finger against her jawline. "I'm great at being a cockblock."

Jay shot his sister a withering look. "I'm well aware. But your cockblock powers are not needed tonight. Avery and I are neighbors who are decorating together. That's it."

Winter shrugged and turned away, busying herself with closing out the register for the day. Jay wanted to believe that everything he was telling his sister was true, but somehow, it didn't feel like it. After the shops closed tonight, the plan was to decorate their stores so that first thing tomorrow morning they would open to participants on the store crawl contest.

Pugs & Kisses had already had some Halloween decor up for weeks, given that Halloween was this coming weekend. But that wasn't Jay's style, and doing this joint venture was already enough of a departure from his norm. Over the next three days, customers would come to their storefront and utilize the Yule Heights Shopping Mall app to vote on their favorite storefronts. On Friday, they'd find out the winners and the prize was—he couldn't believe he was actually excited about this, but he was—dinner for two at La Verde Triste, the only fancy restaurant in town, with a covered tab for a nightcap at The Lucky Leprechaun afterwards.

Oh, and, of course, a congratulatory plaque to put in the storefront window all year long signifying their win.

That part, he could do without.

"Do I need to give you a ride home after we decorate tonight?" Jay asked Winter as he shrugged out of his coat and removed his tie. No point in being in all work attire to do some manual labor around the storefront.

Winter shook her head. "No, I've got a date."

Jay's brows lifted. "You do? With who?"

"This gorgeous lipstick lesbian named Amber who works here part-time during college breaks," Winter mused, her smile widening.

"Works where?" Jay felt prickly, like there should be more to the story.

Winter shrugged. "Here. At the mall."

"Okay, but *where* at the mall?" Jay pushed further, this time tilting his head a bit to the side and staring his sister dead on.

She looked fidgety, and Jay immediately recognized his

sister's tells—she was up to trouble. "Why does it matter? She's just a seasonal worker. It won't get in the way of anything."

"I swear to God, Winter," Jay began. "If she seasonally works at Summer's Sun, you cannot and will not be dating her."

Winter lifted her chin higher in the air, defensiveness crossing her face. "It's part time! And seasonal! Summer would never even know."

Jay shook his head. "That's not true and you know it. You'd *want* Summer to know. The court order was very clear—you have to leave her and Kamar alone. That includes not dating their employees."

"The court order doesn't *actually* say that," Winter argued. "I'm still staying away from the store like I promised."

"I'm driving you home tonight. Period. Cancel the date." Jay didn't wait for her to argue, because he was tired of cleaning up her messes. He loved his sister, but she struggled with mental health issues and she had a very hard time holding boundaries in relationships. He'd only agreed to let her move in with him if she went back on her medication and saw her therapist at least once a week—which, so far, she was doing.

This, however, was a back slide. Jay made a mental note to send Winter's therapist an email tomorrow updating her on this recent development.

"You know we're decorating for Halloween, right? Because you're coming in hot with a Grinch face," Avery commented as he stormed up to them in the corridor in front of their shops. Avery gestured to his expression. "What's happening to your face?"

Their teasing tone lightened Jay's tension a few

millimeters already. He shook his head and ran his hand back through his hair, then rubbed the back of his neck as he cracked it side to side. "Nothing unusual. Just my sister being herself."

Avery seemed to understand that cue and just nodded. "Is she helping us decorate?"

"Maybe." Jay shrugged. "We'll see. In the meantime, let's just get started."

"Okay." Avery pointed to the stack of boxes on two long flatbed metal carts that he'd loaded earlier. Avery must have pulled them out from the back before he'd gotten out here. "I say we start with the big stuff first—the ghosts. Then, we can go back and work on the nuanced details and tangential decor."

"You're the boss," he replied, opening one of the boxes on top to reveal a tall, large stuffed dog. He lifted it out of the box. "Christ, this looks like a real dog."

"It was," Avery commented, taking the dog from him. "He's taxidermized."

"Won't that freak people out?" Although that was kind of the point of Halloween decorations, at least to some extent.

Avery shook their head. "We're covering him with a sheet. He'll be a ghost, and no one's even going to see anything except his eyes and feet."

Jay felt his skin crawl, but then opened up the next box of sheets that they'd already deemed old enough to cut up and utilize for their ghosts. They worked mostly quietly and steadily for the next twenty minutes as Jay set up the glasses-wearing, human-sized ghost wrapped around a mannequin they'd borrowed from the Macy's on one end of the mall. Avery then finished their taxidermy-dog-ghost with a leash leading to Jay's ghost.

Winter came out a few minutes later, carrying the sign that they'd have next to the ghost-and-ghost-dog duo about Companion Canines, a local nonprofit organization that trained and donated highly skilled service dogs to people with visual disabilities. The sign told people where to donate, how to help, and ways that they could volunteer.

Jay stood back, a bit proud of their work. It honestly looked very real, like either one would move at any moment, but it wasn't garish or scary. Instead, it was suspenseful, educational, and—dare he say—professional.

"Okay, time for the fringe decor," Avery announced, clapping their hands together.

Out came a giant spider web from the next box and Jay got up on a ladder to help pin the web above their store signs so that it would drop all the way down to the floor. Avery busied themself with little 3-D bat stickers on both storefront windows that depending on the angle someone viewed from, would seem like they were flying. Last, but not least, were a few more ghost friends in both storefront windows to bring the entire look together.

"Where'd Winter go?" Avery asked as Jay stepped back with them to survey the entire thing.

Jay glanced toward his storefront, and he could see the light to the office in the back was on. "Probably in my office. She's not too pleased with me right now."

"Big brother problems?" Avery prompted, though Jay didn't really feel like answering. "The decorations look good, at least."

"Do you think it's enough to win?" Jay walked to one side and then the other, looking for any gaps in the theme. Honestly, though, it did look really good. There was a spookiness to it that wasn't over-the-top, so it felt like families and kids would still enjoy it. Plus, he really liked the message they were spreading and being able to help an organization that deserved it on top of all that.

Avery had their phone out and was snapping pictures of the displays. "If wholesome is one of the criteria we're being judged on, then absolutely. If not, I'm pretty sure the burned-to-a-crisp zombie climbing out of the tanning bed at Summer's Sun might beat us."

"Way to think positive." Jay chuckled. "I think we've got a real shot."

"Well, it would be my first time then." Avery came to a stop next to him, tucking their phone back in their pocket. "This mall does so many contests and I'm always trying to win at least one—but no luck yet."

That surprised Jay. "What other contests are there?"

"Well, you've obviously got the Independence Games for the 4th of July, the Gratitude Gong Song at Thanksgiving, and the craziest of all, of course, being the New Year, New You Makeover Contest that Barber Streisand's Salon hosts every January." Avery ticked off each contest on one of their fingers. "I think I'm still forgetting some."

"I can't believe I'm the standout weirdo in a place like this," Jay commented, mostly kidding, but also...not really. "This entire mall is absolutely nuts."

"You're not wrong there," Avery agreed. "But maybe that's why you'll fit right in. Weird is open to weird."

Jay adjusted one of the 3-D bats. "I'm not weird, though. My family is."

"Oh, Jay, if there is one thing I can promise you, it is that you are super weird, too." Avery laughed, and their hand squeezed his upper arm. "I mean, hopefully not like criminal weird, but still, you've got your quirks."

Jay turned to face Avery, and given the close proximity of where they'd been standing beside him, he found himself chest to chest with them. Avery's eyes widened just enough to be noticeable, and they swallowed hard...but they didn't take a step back. Neither did Jay. Instead, he let his gaze drop from Avery's eyes to their lips—soft, pink, a perfectly arched Cupid's bow at the top.

Why did he feel this pull toward them, as if he could just reach forward and pull Avery flush against him and kiss them here and now? He couldn't remember the last time he'd felt a connection in any sort of romantic sense to anyone, and why now?

Jay cleared his throat and took a step back. He noticed the look of disappointment in Avery's eyes, but was it really? Or was it pity for the new kid on the block with the sad back story? If there was one thing he couldn't stand, it was people feeling sorry for him.

"It looks like everything is finished," he said, cleaning his throat as he gestured to the decorations around them. "I'd say it's a pretty good job, don't you think?"

Avery turned away from him for a moment, and the air felt thick between them. "Yeah. It'll get us in the running for the win, that's for sure."

"I've, uh...I've got to get Winter home. I'm her ride." Jay rubbed his hand across the back of his neck and then across his jaw line, his beard soft beneath his palm. "I'll see you in the morning?"

"Yep, great." Avery walked away from him without a second look, heading into Pugs & Kisses. They didn't even say goodbye or offer a wave over their shoulder, and Jay couldn't help but feel like he'd done something wrong.

Like maybe doing nothing in that moment had been wrong.

It felt wrong.

"Ahhhhh!" Winter jumped through the front entrance

to his store with her hands up in the air and blood streaking down her lips and chin and neck.

Jay startled, his hands flying up immediately to defend himself. "Holy shit! What the hell, Winter?"

Winter grinned and then opened her mouth to show a blood pack. "Fake blood. I think we should add an interactive component to the decorations. I'll jump out and go zombie on people."

"Absolutely not." Jay shook his head and walked past her into the store. "Come on, pack your stuff. Let's go home."

Winter sidled up next to him, wiping the fake blood off her face with a napkin. "Okay, but do you want to talk about your hypocrisy first?"

He frowned at his sister as he grabbed the keys to his truck from behind the front desk. "What are you talking about?"

"The canoodling!" Winter wiggled her index finger, pointing from him toward the front entrance. "You and the pet store owner. You said I can't date someone who works at the mall and you're over there basically pawing at them like a stray."

Jay rolled his eyes hard. "No one is pawing at anyone. We're neighbors. That's it."

"Mmmmmkay," Winter dragged out the sound in a long, exaggerated tone. "I know pheromones on fire when I see them. And *that* was an inferno."

He wasn't going to keep entertaining his sister's theatrics, but it did give him slight pause that someone else had noticed the same thing that he had. Was there something there? Was Avery really interested in him romantically? Given everything they knew about him, he couldn't imagine that to be true.

"Listen, Jekyll," Winter began as she followed him out of the store through the back entrance to the parking lot. "Can I give you some advice?"

He locked the store behind them and shook his head. "Absolutely not."

"Well, I'm going to anyway," Winter replied, matching his stride with two quick steps for every one long one of his. "My therapist says I have to stop defining myself by what our mother did. And, you know what, you do it, too."

Jay's jaw clenched. "I don't define any part of myself by that woman."

"Sure, sure. But, let's say you did. If you did, then you might see yourself as an extension of her, and, well, I love mom but at best she abandoned us because she wouldn't tell the truth about dad and at worst, she killed him." Winter was ticking off the options on her fingers like it was a completely normal conversation despite Jay's grimace as he unlocked the truck and opened the passenger door for his sister. "Either way, my therapist said that we can't keep living in her shadow. We're not her, and we deserve love and happiness."

"You're *not* going out with Amber," Jay reminded her as he climbed into his side of the cab and started the truck. "If that's where this diatribe is going."

"This isn't about me, dick face," Winter scoffed. "It's about you. You've been single for...for literally ever. You clearly have a connection with Avery. Why stop yourself?"

Jay didn't respond, but instead turned on the radio.

Winter automatically groaned at his choice of radio station. "Can't you drown me out with something more modern? This music is like twenty-five years old. I wasn't even born when it came out."

He turned the music up louder.

# CHAPTER SIX

## AVERY

"This is incredible," the volunteer representative from Companion Canines told Avery as he surveyed the front of the store. "What a unique idea. Can I take a picture to post on our Instagram?"

"Of course!" Avery gestured toward the decorations that they had set up last night with Jay as they petted the head of a beautiful Labrador retriever that was with the representative. "Hopefully, this can help bring in some donations."

"We've already had one hundred and fifty dollars donated this morning through your donation link," he informed them. The dog he was training sat down on his haunches and yawned. "So, with three more days of this being up before Halloween, I can imagine it's going to help a lot."

"Wow! That was fast." Avery felt pleased that their efforts were already beginning to pay off, even if just in small increments. They saw Jay passing through his storefront and waved him over. "Here, I want you to meet Dr. Jekyll Storm. He's the other person running this with me."

Jay walked toward them in a white doctor's coat and immediately put his hand out for the dog, but the dog didn't move until the representative gave it a head nod. "Wow, that dog is well trained."

"Jay, this is Stevie from Companion Canines," Avery introduced the representative to him. "Stevie, this is Storm Optical Care's owner, Dr. Jekyll Storm. This entire theme was mostly his idea."

"Call me Jay." He put his hand out toward the representative. "Avery just loves to remind people of my full name around this holiday."

Stevie laughed lightly. "It is quite thematic. Your mom really went all out for Halloween."

"You have no idea." Jay grinned, and Avery couldn't help but notice he seemed lighter than usual—after all, he had just made a joke about his jailed mother. Maybe it was because he was currently petting the dog and clearly fawning over him, but whatever it was, he seemed happy in that moment and that wasn't an emotion they'd seen on him before. "Thanks for allowing us to spotlight your organization for this. It's really great to be able to turn this whole contest thing into a meaningful purpose. Hell, it's the only way Avery got me on board."

"You know, we're always looking for people to help train one of our dogs. It can take anywhere from three months to two years, depending on the dog and the trainer." Stevie looked between Jay and the Labrador. "If that's ever something you'd be interested in, I'd love to get you set up with one of our volunteer coordinators."

"I don't know anything about training dogs," Jay quickly said, standing up straighter. "Believe me, I'd be no good at it."

Stevie waved a hand like it was no big deal. "We'll train

you how to do it and have a coordinator working with you every step of the way. You'd start with a puppy living with you and just basic puppy training, and then once fully trained for service work, we'd pair the dog with someone with disabilities who desperately needs it but can't afford the cost of buying one themselves."

There was a flicker of concern in Jay's eyes, but he didn't seem entirely opposed to the idea.

"Didn't you say Winter's been talking about getting a dog?" Avery added, gesturing between them. "Maybe this is fate."

Jay shot them a look. "And I told Winter no just the same. Dogs are big commitments."

"So is owning a business, or building relationships, or being alive," Avery pointed out. "And look at you—doing all those things like a professional."

Avery didn't miss the smirk on Jay's lips at the emphasis they put on the last word.

Stevie handed Jay a card anyway. "No worries. Take your time. Think it over. If you ever change your mind, reach out to me. No pressure either way."

"I mean, I'll apply pressure," Avery tossed in, but then the moment the words left their mouth, they realized that could be taken in a sexual manner. "Metaphorically, of course. About the dog."

The corners of Jay's lips twitched into the smallest of smiles. "You seem to see everything as a challenge."

Avery shrugged their shoulders. "Makes life more fun."

Stevie said his goodbyes and headed out to the main corridor of the mall. Several groups of mall patrons came by, all holding the score cards for the Halloween Contest Crawl.

"Are you two the owners?" A woman in a light green

shirt and dark jeans pointed toward both stores and then at Avery and Jay. "I definitely want to vote for you guys this year."

"We are!" Avery beamed, linking their arm around Jay's elbow. "Thank you so much!"

"It's an amazing idea. My sister is blind and her dog is the biggest part of helping her live an independent life," the woman continued, taking her phone out to snap a photo of the non-profit's information on the sign. "I'll be donating to Canine Companions as well."

"That's really generous," Jay added, glancing down at their arm linked around his. "It's nice to hear a success story like that."

"Have you two ever trained a seeing-eye dog before?" the woman continued, putting the phone back in her jeans pocket. "You guys are such a cute couple. I imagine you probably have several babies running around, but a dog is a great project for kids to help with as well!"

Avery grinned and let out a small chuckle, but then was quickly jostled by Jay yanking his arm away from them and taking several steps to the side to place distance between them.

"We are *not* a couple," Jay assured the stranger. The emphasis he put on the words felt aggressive. Hurtful? They weren't sure why they were reacting to his statement, but something in their chest felt heavy. Strange, because they'd been about to say the same thing to the woman. After all, they were not a couple. That was the fact.

So why did it feel so bad when he said it out loud?

Avery frowned and cleared their throat. "Uh, right. We're not together. Just neighbors."

"It's a completely professional relationship," Jay added to the end of their sentence.

They shot him an annoyed look. "I think we've made our point."

The woman looked between them with an uncomfortable grimace. "Uh, sorry about that. You guys just looked so comfortable together. I shouldn't have assumed."

With that, the woman basically sprinted down the hallway to the main corridor to escape them.

"Well, I hope she still votes for us after you just made that incredibly awkward," Avery snapped out at Jay, their arms crossed over their chest. "You might have just cost us a donation."

Jay had a deer-in-headlights look to him. "I was just telling the truth."

Avery rolled their eyes. "I know."

"So, why are you upset?" There was a twinge of defensiveness in his tone now, and Avery sighed, not wanting this to become a conflict despite the surge of emotions they were feeling right then.

"I'm not," Avery bit back. "It's fine. Everything is fine. I have to go to work."

With that, they turned on their heel and walked back inside Pugs & Kisses. Although *walked* might not be as accurate of a term as *stomped*. They definitely stomped back into the store and stormed to the back office where Lizzy was standing on a chair with her arms lifted above her.

"Ah!" Lizzy startled at the sound of Avery banging open the back-office door. "Quick! Close the door!"

Avery shut the door behind them fast. "What's going on?"

Lizzy gave her a puzzled look, and Avery realized the irritation and anger was still in their voice. "Pete Davidson got out of his cage."

Pete Davidson was a parrot who had a side hustle as an escape artist that they'd been trying to sell for over a year now, but it seemed he might just be a permanent fixture at the store now.

Avery glanced up toward the ceiling that was industrial style and not closed off, so it was just a ton of pipes and open space. "How long has he been out?"

"I've been trying to trap him for about ten minutes now." Lizzy shook her head and sighed as she jumped down from chair and onto the floor. "But he can wait. What the hell's going on with you?"

"What do you mean? I'm fine." Avery gritted out the word so hard that even they didn't believe them. "I mean... fine-ish."

Lizzy lifted one brow, both hands on her hips. "Spill."

"It's really nothing," Avery assured her, taking a seat in one of the old office chairs and letting out a sigh. "I mean, it's hard to even explain. I don't really know why I'm upset. Jay said something to a customer and it just struck a wrong chord with me."

"That dick face." Lizzy took a seat next to them. "What did he say? I'll go march right over there now and make him apologize."

Avery grinned, feeling a little lighter with Lizzy's aggressive humor. "I promise, it was nothing. He just told a customer that we weren't together."

"Like he tried to take credit for the decorations by himself?" Lizzy's eyes went huge. "He said he did all that without you? Oh, yeah, you have every right to be upset. How could he take credit for all that when it was your idea?"

Avery shook their head. "No, I mean...he said we weren't together, like, romantically. Like a couple."

Lizzy paused and Avery could see the wheels turning in her head. "But...you're not together. Are you? Did I black out and miss a boyfriend? Holy crap, I really need to start cutting back on my nightly bottle of wine."

"Of course we're not together. We are definitely, one hundred percent not dating," Avery confirmed. "And also... a bottle every night? Girl."

"It's my daily serving of fruit!" Lizzy defended herself. "Plus, I get the low-calorie bottles and then it's basically like water, you know. I'm staying hydrated."

Avery laughed and shook their head but made a mental note to check in on Lizzy more often. "Whatever you say."

"Hey, don't change the subject." Lizzy pointed at them now. "We're talking about you and what is clearly a crush you have on Dr. Dick next door."

"I do not have a crush on Jay," Avery responded so quickly that they nearly cut Lizzy off.

Lizzy gave them a knowing look. "Thou doth protest too much. Why does it bother you if he says you're not together, then? I mean, you're *not*."

"I knoooow!" Avery dragged out the word as they released a long breath. "Honestly, I don't know. I have no idea why I'm upset. Let's just forget this and catch Pete Davidson."

"That damn bird," Lizzy commented, glancing up at the ceiling where they could both see him sitting on top of one of the metal airducts that ran the length of the office. "I think we'll have to bribe him down with treats."

"You know the only thing that's really going to work," Avery commented, lifting their brows and grinning at Lizzy. "You're going to have to sing to him his favorite song."

"But he *hates* my singing," Lizzy whined. "He'll attack me!"

"Yeah, but then I can grab him." Avery was fully aware they were asking their employee to put herself in parrot-claw danger, but a Taylor Swift song—and only a Taylor Swift song—was going to bring Pete Davidson down to hand-grabbing levels and they both knew it.

"Ugh." Lizzy huffed, tapping her foot. "Okay, but I'm changing the lyrics."

Avery shrugged. "I mean, I don't think he understands the actual lyrics. Go for it."

Lizzy took a deep breath and began singing to the melody of You Need to Calm Down by Taylor Swift. "Oh-oh, oh-oh, oh-oh, oh-oh, oh-oh, you need to come down! You're being too proud! And I'm just like oh-oh, oh-oh, oh-oh, oh-oh, you need to just drop, like can you just stop being an ass, you need to come down!"

Lizzy had barely gotten the last word out when Pete Davidson swooped in with a vengeance clearly ready to claw her eyes out. He never got the opportunity, of course, because Avery grabbed him the moment he was within arm's reach and skillfully put him back inside his cage.

"See!" Lizzy pointed accusatorially at the parrot. "He tried to kill me. Adim gets to clean his cage from now on. Pete Davidson and I are done."

"You sound like a Kardashian," Avery teased. "But sure, I'll ask Adim to be on Pete duty for the next week."

"Month," Lizzy corrected. "My heart needs time to heal from this break up."

Avery rolled their eyes and laughed, picking up the cage and carefully carrying it back out to the showroom floor where it normally sat. They placed him carefully in his spot and glanced through the cage to see Jay still standing in front of his store where they'd left him.

He was staring in their direction, and he looked

conflicted as he stared at something in his hand. Avery narrowed their eyes slightly and focused in on the small black item in his hand—it was a fucking cricket. They quickly turned around and busied themself with another task because they didn't have time to sit and puzzle on why they'd reacted the way they had earlier or to deal with being blamed for all the loose crickets throughout Yule Heights.

Nor did they have time to wonder why Jay was staring at them like he was having some kind of emotionally unclear reaction of his own.

# CHAPTER SEVEN

### JAY

"It's been two days of this," Winter pointed out to Jay as she leaned against the reception counter in Storm Optical Care. "You can't be dressed as a vampire *and* be moping. That's like Twilight shit. Might as well go cry in the forest and forget where you are."

"What the hell are you talking about?" Jay pulled the fake plastic vampire teeth out of his mouth so he could talk more easily. "I'm not moping, and I have never watched Twilight."

Winter shrugged her shoulders and Jay knew a scathing snap back was coming. "Wouldn't know it by the way you're all vampire-y moping over an unrequited love. That's basically the entire plot."

"There's no unrequited love in my life, believe me," he assured his sister.

She lifted one brow. "Well, that's cocky. Someone assumes they just can get anyone they set their eyes on? Maybe that's why you're still single."

"I'm still single because I choose to be, thank you very much." Jay huffed and tucked the fake teeth into the interior pocket of the red and black vampire cape he'd tied around his neck. His hair was slicked back with gel, and he'd even gone a step further to put on black eyeliner around his eyes and drops of fake blood in his beard to really sell the look. "It wasn't exactly easy getting this place up and running. Work had to be my focus, not dating."

"And now that it is already up and running?" Winter asked, her arms folded across each other on the counter now as she gave him a pointed look. "You're ready to start dating again?"

"I didn't say that," Jay countered, though he didn't have any valid facts to back up why he shouldn't.

It wasn't that he wasn't interested in dating—in fact, it would be really nice to have someone to come home to who wasn't his sister. But moving back to his hometown had put him on the defensive, and he couldn't imagine creating a dating profile and being swiped on by people who might know who his mother was. It wasn't exactly a great ice breaker for love.

"Great, because I think I should be in charge of your Tinder profile," Winter offered. "I'm really great on those apps. Also, I should write your bio because you're not great with words."

Jay shot his sister a look. "Absolutely the fuck not. I'm not doing Tinder—or any dating app. I'm not interested in just randomly swiping on people. I can't form a real connection with someone that way."

Winter grinned and wiggled her brows. "So then ,would you say that working together to create a two-store co-decorated Halloween theme for a good cause is a great way to form a real connection?"

"Why are you pushing for this so hard?" Jay glanced

down at his schedule for when the next appointment was coming in. "You can focus on your own love life, you know."

"That's not been my area of expertise," Winter reminded him. "But at least I get out there and try. I know I'm worthy of love and I'm looking for it. You've just given up and decided that because of who we are—or who we're related to—you can't or won't or shouldn't find love. I don't know which it is, but I know that it makes me sad. Because if you believe that about you, then I should believe that about me, too."

Jay looked up at Winter, and for the first time, he noted real vulnerability in her eyes. "Winter, I do not think you're not worthy of love. I know this last year has been trying for you with everything that happened with Summer, but you've been doing the work to get better and grow. Everyone is worthy of love—especially you."

She tilted her head to the side just an inch. "Everyone includes you too, big brother."

"It does," he confirmed, though the words didn't feel as true on his lips as when he'd said them to Winter. Did he not believe that? Did he think he wasn't worthy of love because of his family history? That sounded sad to admit to himself. "I'm just slower to warm up."

Winter was quiet for a few moments. "Do you ever visit her?"

He knew immediately that Winter was referring to their mother, and that she already knew the answer to her question was a resounding no. Not once had he ever visited her in prison, nor had he even remotely wanted to. He looked away and didn't respond.

"I did. Last month," Winter admitted, continuing despite his silence. "She's...she's softer now. I'm not sure how, but she just seems more genteel. Meeting her now, it would be impossible to think that she did what she did."

"She killed him, Winter," Jay reminded her. "She killed our father. We grew up without a father because of her."

"We also grew up without a mother because of her," Winter added, not arguing. "But we grew up with each other. For what it's worth, I couldn't have done it without you and if there's anyone in the world who deserves to feel the full spectrum of love, it's you. You gave it to me."

Jay didn't know how to respond to his sister in that moment without showing more emotion than he was comfortable with, so, instead, he just nodded and looked away. "My next appointment will be here in a minute. Text me when they get here. I've got some paperwork to finish up in the back."

Winter nodded, staring at him with a calmness he hadn't seen in her in a while. Despite the stress his sister's actions often caused him, there was a good, deep soul under the chaos. That was kind of their family crest if he really thought about it. *Wade through the muck and you'll find the diamond.* But who really wanted to wade through all his muck?

Avery's face came to mind, but he tried to push it away immediately. No luck, though, as he thought of how they'd reacted a few days ago when he'd told a customer that they weren't a couple. Which *was* the truth after all, so at first, he'd just been really confused as to why they'd seemed so upset. He'd seen them this morning on his walk in—Avery was dressed as a ringmaster from a circus, and he'd gotten a little laugh out of that. Not that he'd told them. In fact, he'd gone out of his way to circumvent where they were standing so that he wouldn't run into them.

Jay finished with the rest of his clients as efficiently as

he could, schedule-wise. It was exactly the distraction he needed to keep out of his head throughout the day. That was, until Mara walked into the front of his store at the end of the shift with Avery right behind her. And by right behind her, he meant that Mara was literally dragging Avery by their wrist with what seemed like much hesitation on Avery's part.

"Jay!" Mara shouted, looking for him as he walked out of the back office.

"Everything okay?" He frowned as he walked up to the two of them.

"Does my smile look like everything is okay?" Mara asked, her face lit up into a grin as wide as the Cheshire Cat. "Because it is. Everything is okay. More than okay!"

"I have no idea what she's talking about," Avery added, yanking their wrist out of their sister-in-law's hand. "She just barged into the store and dragged me here."

Jay and Avery both turned to look at Mara.

"You won!" Mara shouted, jumping up in the air.

Winter popped her head out from behind the receptionist desk. "We won?"

Mara nodded enthusiastically as she turned to where Winter was standing. "Both of your stores won—combined, you guys doubled the score of even the first runner up. I mean, it wasn't even a close contest!"

Avery's eyes grew huge and their brows lifted nearly to their hairline. "What?"

Jay pulled out his phone from his pocket and checked the donation tracker website. They'd already hit their target goal of a thousand dollars and then some...in fact, a lot of some. "Holy shit, we're at eighteen hundred dollars in donations."

"See?" Mara pointed toward the screen of his phone.

"You guys were a hit. Here's your prize. I hope you guys enjoy! I'm going to take some photos of the display for social media."

She pulled an envelope out of the back pocket of her jeans and handed it to Jay.

He took it, turning it over and then handing it off to Avery. "Here. It was your idea. You can have it."

Mara shook her head. "No, it's a gift for two."

Avery glanced suspiciously at their sister-in-law as they tore open the envelope and pulled out a certificate inside. "Dinner and drinks for two at...oh my God, to La Verdad Triste? That place is super expensive."

"Plus, a night cap at The Lucky Leprechaun after." Mara grinned at both of them. "I made you reservations for tonight—so get ready, because they expect you both there in thirty minutes."

"Mara!" Avery scoffed. "I have to finish closing up the store. Lizzy is there alone right now."

"I'll help her," Winter volunteered. "We're already closed up over here. I'll help Lizzy close and you two go eat."

"In costume?" Jay glanced down at his vampire outfit. "I mean, if it's a fancy restaurant, shouldn't we be dressed up?"

Mara shook her head and then shook the grass skirt she was wearing around her hips over her jeans. "Nope. It's Halloween! Costumes are expected everywhere in Yule Heights."

"Do you even want to go?" Avery cast him a long look. "Together, I mean. You were pretty insistent about that earlier."

Jay tensed, but he wasn't dodging this question. "I'd like to go, Avery."

They seemed to be surveying him for truthfulness. "Okay. I mean, I guess we'll go. It's a free dinner."

"See you kids tomorrow!" Mara stated, turning to head out of the store. "Have fun!"

"I'll, uh, just go talk to Lizzy really quick and then I'll meet you back here? We can carpool?" Avery suggested.

Jay nodded, because that certainly made the most sense. "Sure. I'll wait for you here."

The shiver of excitement rolling up his spine wasn't lost on him. Was this a date? Of course, it wasn't. But did he want it to be? The nervous energy tingling across his limbs said yes.

# CHAPTER EIGHT

## AVERY

"Wow. This place really is fancy," Jay said as he held open the front door to La Verde Triste and Avery walked through, their full ringmaster costume leaving little bits of glitter on the floor with each step they took.

"It's the fanciest place in town," Avery confirmed as they waited in a small queue of people next to a wide mirror on the wall. Avery pointed at their reflection in the mirror. "Hey, where'd you go?"

"What?" Jay looked at the two of them in the mirror, completely missing the reference.

Avery gave him a pointed look. "It was a vampire joke. Because you're dressed like a vampire."

He frowned. "I don't get it. Are vampires invisible or something?"

With a dramatic flair, Avery put their hand in front of their face and rubbed the spot between their brows. "You're dressed as a vampire for Halloween and you don't even know that vampires don't have a reflection?"

He glanced back at the two of them in the mirror. "Oh, so I'm invisible in the mirror."

"This is going to be a long dinner," Avery commented, mostly as a joke but they noted he flinched slightly at that comment. They felt a stirring of remorse, wishing they could pull those words back. "I mean, I'm looking forward to it. The food here is great."

"Yeah." Jay's tone was empty as they stepped up to the host stand and he told the hostess their party's name.

The hostess picked up two menus and motioned for them to follow her as she led them to a darker, more obscure part of the restaurant where a half-circle red booth with a curtain that pulled open or draped closed offered them more privacy.

Avery felt their skin prickling with nerves. Hiding behind a curtain with a non-self-aware vampire at a fancy restaurant felt very intimate, and they were still holding on to the sting from a few days ago. *We're not together.* Although, they still weren't entirely sure why that sentence had stung so much, or why they'd found themself trying to catch a peek of Jay through his store window over the last few days. Something inside them was drawing them closer to him, and it felt terrifying.

He was damaged goods. Period. Avery knew that. Hell, everyone in Yule Heights knew that. But somehow, that only fed their fire rather than extinguished it.

Probably something to bring up with their therapist at some point.

Jay gestured for Avery to pick their seat first, so they slid into the booth on the right side until they were close to the middle. Jay did the same from the opposite direction so now they were seated next to each other, but with enough space and angling to also be partially facing each other as well.

The hostess handed them both their menus and assured them the server would be over shortly to take their order.

Avery lifted the menu in front of them like a shield they could hide behind. That only worked for about thirty seconds, however, since they were a historically fast decision maker and knew almost instantly what they were going to order off the menu.

"What are you going to get?" they asked Jay.

He shrugged, continuing to scan the menu. "I always have a hard time committing to just the right one. It all looks so good, you know?"

Avery tried not to internally sigh, but they felt that answer in their bones. Of course, he struggled with commitment. "Kind of a slogan for your life, huh?"

He glanced up at them over the top of the menu, a glaze of guilt crossing his eyes before he dropped them back to the menu. "Not with everything."

Something about that comment felt like an open door, but Avery didn't walk through.

The server came and introduced himself a moment later, taking their drink orders—mojito for Avery and a gin neat for Jay—as well as an appetizer order before leaving them alone again. The server was wearing cat ears as his Halloween costume, and Avery couldn't help but smile that the holiday spirit of this town could even permeate a stuffy place like this.

"I know the impression I give off." Jay's words were quiet, and he was looking down at his hands as he spoke. "You're not the first person to point it out to me."

Avery felt a seed of guilt in their gut. "I didn't mean to point anything out," they assured him. "It's fine. We're fine. Hey, we're celebrating."

Jay didn't take the bait for a change of topic. "It's not, though. Fine, I mean. The version of me you've seen isn't who I want to be."

Avery was quiet for a few moments, unsure if they should respond or wait for him to further explain.

"I'd actually been seeing a therapist before returning to Yule Heights," Jay continued. "Haven't found one here I've connected with yet, but previously, I did a lot of work on the walls I put up around me. Why I put them there in the first place, how they've helped me survive, and also how they've held me back and made me miss out on people and moments that might have really added to my life in a positive way."

The server returned at that moment with their drinks, and they both sat quietly for a moment until he left. Jay sipped the edge of his glass as Avery did the same, keeping their body angled toward him hoping to invite him to keep sharing if he wanted. They were afraid if they spoke, if they said something to ruin his momentum, he'd clam right back up and this felt like a moment he really needed.

He continued. "Despite doing that work in the therapy space, it's something entirely different going out into the real work and actually putting it into practice—with real people, with you."

"Me?" Avery lifted their brows in surprise.

Jay nodded and his eyes found theirs. "It's been a long time since I've wanted to let someone in past those walls, and I honestly have no idea if that's something you even want to be part of. I fully realize I might be completely shooting in the dark right now."

"You're not." The words came out of Avery's mouth before they could even register that they'd said them.

He looked surprised and cautious all at the same time, and with a slow nod he continued. "I know we're here because we won this dinner, and I don't want you to think I had ulterior motivations this entire time. I really did enjoy the work we did together, and it felt incredibly meaningful to make a difference for an organization that works so hard for the people they help. But, if you're open to it, I'd like this to not be our last dinner together."

Avery picked up their drink and took a larger gulp this time. Their mind was spinning with the possibilities Jay was presenting to them in that moment. Did they want this? Did they want him? The answer had felt obvious days ago when his perceived rejection had stung so deeply, but he wasn't rejecting them right now.

Instead, he was asking to be accepted.

"You're throwing me a bit for a loop here, Jay," Avery admitted, placing their drink back down on the table.

He did the same and turned to angle his body even more towards them, his knee now propped up on the booth seat between them. "I know. I'm kind of freaking out right now."

Avery glanced up at his face and took in, for the first time, his expression. Sheer panic. Stoic panic. Like he was clearly very uncomfortable with everything he was saying, and yet he was saying it anyway. He was sitting in his discomfort and just allowing his offer to hang between them without trying to run away.

Deciding to meet him where he was at, Avery also turned to face him and angled their knee up on the booth seat. "You've got that deer in headlights look going on."

"And you still haven't answered my question," Jay added.

"My older brother, Val, is a lot like you in some ways," Avery responded, skirting around his probe. "And, as the younger sister, it was really hard to live up to him and his success. Everything he did was perfect and put on a pedestal and I was always the odd one out. When I came out as nonbinary in my teenage years, my parents were supportive, but they never really took the time to understand. They never tried to do the research or ask the questions that would have helped them really get to know me for who I am—not just as their daughter."

Jay placed his hand on their knee and left it there. It was strangely comforting.

"Val was always a die-hard romantic—just like my parents. They had a fairytale type of love, and still do to this day. Me, however...." Avery exhaled slowly and then filled their lungs again. "I think I felt like I slipped into the background. Like I disappeared or wasn't seen...and a few days ago in the mall when you pulled away from me and said we weren't together—which I know, we weren't—but I think it hit a trigger for me. It felt like I wasn't being seen...again."

Jay squeezed their knee and lightly ran his thumb back and forth across the skin on the inner side of their leg. "I can see why it would have felt that way, but the truth is that I've seen nothing but you since I got here. And I can't turn away."

Avery's breath hitched in their throat as they looked down at his hand on their knee.

"And I think the scariest part," Jay continued. "Is that you so clearly see me. And you don't hide it. You don't sugarcoat your punches. You tell me exactly what you see, and I'm not sure I've ever loved seeing myself. But something about the way you see me, the way I feel reflected through your eyes...it doesn't feel as awful as it used to."

They were both quiet for a moment before Avery placed their hand on Jay's and intertwined their fingers with his.

"Ask me again," Avery prompted, squeezing his fingers tightly for a quick moment. "Ask me for another dinner."

A hesitant and clearly nervous smile lifted the corners of Jay's lips and his free hand rubbed his beard across his jaw line. "Avery, do you want to go out to dinner again with me?"

"I'm free tomorrow night," they responded, smiling wider.

The tension in Jay's brows seemed to dissipate, and he leaned forward ever so slightly. "Can I ask one more question?"

Avery nodded as the server dropped off their appetizer and quickly scurried away to leave them alone.

He inhaled slowly, as if steadying himself. "Can I kiss you?"

Avery nodded again, but then didn't wait. Instead, they leaned forward and met Jay the rest of the way, placing their lips to his. He seemed frozen for a split second, but then melted into them in a way that simply felt...safe. His hand left their knee and, instead, his arms wrapped around their waist and pulled them closer to him.

Avery felt lost, but this time in an entirely different way. Lost in him. Lost in this kiss. Lost in the promise and hope it held for what might be coming next. Who they might become next. And somehow, that sort of lost made them feel more visible than anything ever had before.

He saw them, and they'd waded through the muck to find the diamond he was hiding.

A ringmaster and a vampire kissing in a booth...sometimes the best Halloween love stories begin with a haunted past.

# EPILOGUE
## AVERY

"I can't believe this day is finally here," Jay admitted as they walked through the front doors of the Canine Companion main headquarters.

Avery squeezed his forearm supportively. "You've done an incredible job with Steve Buscemi. His new owner is going to be so incredibly blessed after everything you've trained him to do."

Jay glanced at them and nodded, but Avery saw the hint of tears in the corners of his eyes. When he'd first agreed last year to take in and train a puppy for Canine Companion, Avery had been shocked. When they'd first started dating, Jay had been anti-dog and it seemed to be such a solid stance, there was no way of changing it. But they'd done a few more volunteer events with the organization and something changed his mind—he signed up.

At first, Avery had been worried they'd get too attached to the puppy and it would hurt too much to say goodbye. It became quickly apparent, however, that the opposite was the case. Steve Buscemi moved in with them a month after Avery had moved into Jay's house—and Winter had moved out. Not that they'd kicked her out. No, Winter was doing really well in a prestigious internship in New York City to become a makeup artist. She was chasing her dreams, and Avery and Jay had both been happy to send her off with good vibes.

"Dr. Jekyll!" Stevie walked out of the back office with his arms raised. "Good to see you again, man."

"It's Jay," Jay reminded him for the umpteenth time.

Stevie grinned, and round and round the two went with this charade where Stevie always pretended to forget. "How's my namesake?"

"Again, not your namesake." Jay huffed, but Avery could see he wasn't actually upset. "Steve Buscemi is a hero and a firefighter, and this dog is going to be every bit the hero he's named after."

"Hey, I've been heroic a time or two," Stevie defended himself with an even wider grin. "I always bring the cart back at the grocery store instead of leaving it in the parking lot."

Jay rolled his eyes, then got down on one knee to pet dog Steve. Now a year and a half old, Steve Buscemi was a beautiful golden retriever with red hues to his fur and a gentle, mild manner that would serve him well with his new owner. Jay had seen to that.

"We're going to miss him," Avery told Steve. "He's such an incredible dog. When is the family going to be here?"

"They're actually waiting in my office now. Are you guys ready?" Steve motioned back to his office. "Or do you want a few minutes to say goodbye?"

"We already said our goodbyes," Jay told him, standing back up. His jaw was set firm, and Avery slipped their hand in his with another small squeeze.

Dating this man for two years had been more than

enough time to see beneath his tough exterior, but when things got hard emotionally, his walls still went up sky high. They could see him doing it now, and honestly, they didn't blame him. Saying goodbye to Steve Buscemi was one of the harder things Avery had had to do as well, and they'd only peripherally been involved in his training.

"Then come on back," Steve said, ushering them toward his office. He led the way and opened the door, and Steve Buscemi walked through first, tail wagging.

When Avery and Jay entered, they found themselves in what looked to be a large living room but with a desk to one side. There were two large couches facing one another and a family of three sat on the one furthest from the door.

Avery surveyed them as both of them sat in the opposite couch, Steve Buscemi's leash still wrapped around Jay's arm. The father was older—his hair and beard already completely white and a tired look to his eyes that seemed kind yet overwhelmed. Next to him was a young boy, couldn't have been older than eleven or twelve, though Avery wasn't an expert on kids or guessing ages. He was holding a white cane with a few red lines on it, tucked between his legs and playing with a stray thread on the knee of his jeans. Next to the young boy was who they assumed to be the boy's mother. Her hair was pulled back into a tight and high ponytail and she was in all athletic leisure wear with a large binder in her lap that had a ton of tabs sticking out of the side. She had a more youthful look than the father, but the furrow on her brows spoke of anxiety.

"Good morning," the mother broke the silence first. She stood and reached out a hand to Avery and then Jay. "I'm Jessi and this is my husband, Scott. Our son here is Benjamin."

Benjamin looked up at them and smiled widely, but his

gaze didn't seem to connect with either of them. "Is the dog here?"

Jay was standing after shaking Jessi's hand and walked Steve Buscemi over to the other side of the couch, instructing him to sit in front of Benjamin. "He is, Benjamin. This is Steve Buscemi. Named after a heroic firefighter during 9/11 and, of course, the famous actor, he's going to help guide you going forward. Would you like to pet him?"

Benjamin nodded, his grin still wide as he reached out his hand.

Jay guided his hand to Steve Buscemi's back and the young boy's fingers sank into the dog's soft fur. He ran his hand down the length of the dog's back and then up to find his head. Steve Buscemi sat patiently and quietly as Benjamin felt him, letting him explore his face and snout and ears without so much as a whimper.

"He's so soft," Benjamin said. "And big!"

"He might still grow a little more," Jay informed the family. "He's only one and a half years old, but he's pretty close to his full height and weight most likely."

"I can't tell you how much this means to our family," Jessi said, her eyes on her son. "We've been on the list for three years, and to finally get Benjamin the companion helper he needs feels so amazing. I worry about him at school and places where I can't be there around the clock, you know? As he's getting older, that's happening a lot more than I was ready for. Knowing Steve Buscemi is going to be with him all the times that I'm not..." Jessi let out a long sigh, and her entire body seemed to relax. "It's a big gift you've given us."

Jay smiled and sat back down on the couch next to Avery. They could see his smile didn't reach his eyes, but they didn't push. "Thanks, I appreciate it. He was an easy dog to train. A lot of it really came naturally to him."

"Incredible," Steve added from where he was standing watching the entire interaction. "Again, we'd love to continue with follow up visits with Steve Buscemi to continue training and making sure he's adapting to all the specific needs Benjamin might have. But aside from that, he's ready to go home with you today."

"Hold on one second," Jay said, getting back to his feet. "I'll be right back."

He left the office and Avery glanced at the family apologetically. "Sorry, I'm not sure what he's doing."

They all sat for a few minutes as Benjamin kept stroking the dog, waiting for Jay to return. When he did, he nearly burst through the office door like he was going to break it down. In his arms was a small cardboard box and he walked it over to Benjamin, placing it on the couch next to the son.

"Here's his box," Jay said, reaching in and pulling items out. "His favorite food bowl—helps him eat slower. He can be very greedy when it comes to food if left unchecked."

Jay placed the bowl in Benjamin's hands and let him feel it.

"And here's his favorite toy. It's a stuffed animal Lamp Chop with squeakers in the paws." Again, Jay placed the item in Benjamin's hands and guided him to where the squeaker was.

Benjamin squeezed it and jolted a little at the loud sound, but then grinned when Steve Buscemi put his chin on his knee, the sound of his tail thumping on the ground unmistakable.

"I also put some of his favorite treats and food in here, and a few other toys. That way he feels at home with you guys." Jay stepped back but didn't rejoin Avery on the couch. "So, yeah. Just...be good to him, you know? He's a really great dog."

Avery heard the strain in Jay's throat and stood, taking his hand. "We should probably get going and give you guys some time to bond."

Jay shot them a grateful look and nodded. "Yeah. Steve has our number if there's ever anything you need. Or if you want to send pictures here and there."

Jessi stood and shook Jay's hand again. "Thank you. Thank you so much."

Avery guided Jay out of the office and back to his truck, but they didn't climb in right away. Instead, Avery pulled Jay into an embrace. "I'm so proud of you, Jay. You just did a really amazing thing for that family."

Jay's arms tightened around their waist and they felt his body tremble against theirs. He didn't respond with words, but they could hear him sniffing, his shoulders shaking slightly as he buried his face in the crook of their neck.

After a few minutes of letting him cry, Avery pulled back and took his face in their hands. Cupping his jaw, they leaned up on their tiptoes and placed a kiss on his lips. He kissed back with a gentleness that told Avery his walls weren't fully up right now. He was allowing himself to feel all of this. He was allowing himself to hurt.

"I love you, Jay," Avery whispered, their hands slipping down to the base of his neck.

Jay smiled and he looked a little less sad. "I love you more. Let's go home."

He wrapped his hand around theirs and walked them to the passenger side of the truck, helping them up like he always did. Avery buckled up as he walked back to the driver's side and then climbed in. He started the truck and looked longingly in the rearview mirror back at the office they'd just left.

"I think I'm ready to finally own a dog," Jay admitted, grinning as he looked sideways at them. "Want to stop by the humane society on the way home?"

Avery grinned. "Let's do it."

*Keep reading for a sample from A Food Court Friendsgiving...*

# RESOURCES ON THE GENDER SPECTRUM

IF YOU'D LIKE to learn more about what nonbinary means, or the gender spectrum in its magnificent entirety, I've provided some resources and research for you below. Please note that while a nonbinary character is included in this book, it is not a coming out story, nor is their gender the focus of the story. It's simply an everyday love story in an everyday world about two human beings that saw a spark in one another.

Because non-binary people get to live normal love stories the same way cisgender people do, without their genitalia or gender identity being the central focus of the story.

PLEASE TAKE the time to review these resources or find your own:

National Center for Transgender Equality (A website): https://transequality.org/issues/resources/understanding-non-binary-people-how-to-be-respectful-and-supportive

. . .

THE LGBT FOUNDATION (A WEBSITE): https://lgbt.
foundation/who-we-help/trans-people/non-binary

THE TREVOR PROJECT (A WEBSITE): https://www.
thetrevorproject.org/resources/article/understanding-
gender-identities/

BEYOND THE GENDER Binary (A book): https://amzn.
to/3eoOAWQ

LIFE ISN'T Binary (A book): https://amzn.to/3epjBK8

# BONUS STORY: A FOOD COURT FRIENDSGIVING

Exclusive Content!

WANT TO READ THE SHORT, short story A Food Court Friendsgiving? You'll find it exclusively in the series long boxset, MALL YEAR LONG, coming November 21,

2022.

<hr>

# A Food Court Friendsgiving
*A Short, Short Story...At the Mall...by Nell*

"LAURA DERN IS NOT INVITED to Friendsgiving," Dash emphatically stated, shaking his head.

Nell's hands propped on her hips and she squared off with her brother, her rosy boa dangling across her shoulders and its carrying case in one hand. "Hey, Friendsgiving is for everyone—all friends. There was nothing about limiting it to a specific species."

"Noelle is barely two years old," Dash reminded her, talking about his daughter with now-wife Chrissy, who also had a son from a previous relationship named Rudy who Dash was very close with. "She's going to freak out and it'll ruin the entire day."

"Or she'll love Laura Dern as much as she does over FaceTime. You guys haven't been back to Yule Heights since she was born, and it's time for Noelle to see where she comes from—snakes and all."

Chrissy was standing behind her husband with a grin on her face. "Dash, I really think it'll be fine. She's got the cage, and Noelle loves Laura Dern when we show her pictures and videos."

Dash stared her down a minute longer and then threw both of his hands up in the air. "Fine. I'm going to go check with Saoirse and Val on the food."

"Ever since Fostering Friends turned into a public

company, he's really been on edge," Chrissy said to Nell once he'd walked off in the direction of the commercial kitchen at the far end of the food court in the Yule Heights Shopping Mall. "It's just a lot of pressure on him, you know?"

Nell smiled at her sister-in-law, loving how she always defended her brother, no matter what. "Or he's just stubborn by nature."

Chrissy laughed. "I'm going to go check on the kids before we get started. I'm sure Mara is tired of holding down the fort even if the cousins are excited to spend time together."

"See you!" Nell waved her off and then headed for the long row of metal cafeteria tables that they'd lined up down the center of the entire food court.

The mall itself was closed until midnight tonight when it would open for Black Friday shoppers—a phenomenon that Nell would never fully understand—but they'd gotten permission from management to host their first annual (hopefully) Friendsgiving here. In the recent years, their family and friend circle around Yule Heights had expanded so much that it was impossible to keep up with everyone all the time and Nell had insisted they do better at getting together.

So, Friendsgiving was born...

KEEP READING *the full epilogue in MALL YEAR LONG!*

ORDER HERE:

https://booksbysarahrobinson.com/books/mall-year-long/

# EXCERPT FROM MALL I WANT FOR CHRISTMAS IS YOU

## A HOLIDAY ROMANCE

# CHAPTER ONE

## DASH

*Ho ho horrible.*

Dash Winters took one look at the frayed velvet red suit that the manager of Yule Heights Shopping Mall was handing him. "It's...um...it's very large."

"Oh, right." The manager turned around and reached into a metal cabinet and pulled out two yellowed pillows without any pillowcases. It was clear that they'd been white once upon a time, but now...not so much.

He grimaced at the mystery stains as the manager also handed him a thick Velcro belt. Honestly, the poor man couldn't have been older than Dash's foster father, but he spoke with a weariness that sounded ancient. "Here. Put the pillow against your stomach and wrap the band around you so it stays put. You'll look as holly jolly as any other mall Santa out there."

"Great." Dash tucked the outfit and pillow under one muscled arm and sidestepped a leak of some mystery liquid from the paneled ceiling. "So, when do I start?"

The harried manager tossed a fake white, curly beard at

Dash which he barely caught in time. "What do you mean? You start now."

"Like *now* now?" Dash had only come in for an interview, but he hadn't expected to get the job immediately. Not that he'd thought competition for mall Santa was all that intense. Especially considering his foster mother had called ahead as city councilwoman to pave the way for him.

He tucked that embarrassing thought away.

"There is already a line of kids waiting, and the Santa we've used the last few years was just arrested for driving under the influence," the manager sat down in his desk chair with a heavy thud. "I can't explain to a bunch of children that Santa drank too much milk with his cookies. So, you're it, kid."

Dash bristled slightly at the term *kid*. He was, after all, twenty-eight years old. Though he knew he had a youthful look to him, it still hit a sore spot. Probably because he had returned to living in his childhood bedroom in his foster parent's house and was now employed full-time—at least for the next twenty-five days—as a mall Santa as a favor to his mother. Despite the unfortunate turn of events his life had taken, he was trying to look at the bright side. This was all for a purpose, and, in the end, it would be worth it.

At least, that's what he hoped.

"Thanks," he replied, pulling the chord for the beard around his neck and letting it hang down like a necklace. "Is there a place I should change?"

The manager didn't even glance up from the computer he was now furiously typing away on. "The employee bathroom is at the end of the hall. The door next to the dumpsters."

*Of course it was.*

Dash nodded and headed out of the small office that

looked more like a converted storage closet. It had absolutely no windows and was off a concrete hallway that ran the length of the mall behind the stores. Random containers or bags of garbage were sitting outside metal doors that were marked with a store's name—most of which he recognized—but then the rest of the hallway was just empty. The off-putting lights above him was missing several bulbs and there was a buzzing sound come from a flickering bulb behind him.

He'd spent most of the last decade in Yule Heights, Michigan, after being placed with his foster parents—who he now considered just his parents—at age sixteen. He'd spent many Friday and Saturday nights loitering around this mall, but it had never occurred to him that there was an intricate behind-the-scenes set up connecting all the stores together and allowing a clear path to the garbage or parking lot without being seen by customers.

The closer he got to his destination, the stronger the smell of garbage was. A small *employee restroom* sign was hanging crookedly from one nail on the back of a door at the end of the hall, and Dash quickly made his way inside and locked it behind him after he switched on the lights.

He turned back around and surveyed the situation. The room was small enough that if he wanted to sit on the toilet and wash his hands at the same time, he certainly could. Dash hung the suit up on the back of the door, praying the rusty hook would hold. The walls were covered in crude drawings, graffiti, and flyers to someone's upcoming garage concert. He smiled slightly when he read the sloppy handwriting on the cracked mirror that said *don't hate me because I'm beautiful, hate me because I fucked your dad.* Someone else had written in another color and handwriting underneath, *go home, mom, you're drunk.*

Okay, so it wasn't all bad.

Dash made quick work of climbing out of his jeans and the ugly Christmas sweater with at least one hundred reindeer on it his mom had insisted he wear stating that it would *nail the spirit of the interview.* To be fair, she'd been right. The manager had taken one look at him and hired him on the spot.

The red pants for the Santa suit hung loosely around his legs, despite the fact that he had generally pretty thick thighs and calves. He spent one to two hours a day working out at the Planet Fitness on the other side of the mall since he didn't have much else to do with his time these days.

Another part of the reason his mother had demanded he get a job and get out of the house.

His phone started buzzing from the pocket of his discarded jeans. He fished it out and hit the answer button, accepting the video call from his older foster sister, Nell, as he propped the phone up on the bathroom sink.

"Oh, God." Nell immediately groaned through the phone. Her bright purple hair was tossed over her shoulder and he could tell from the background behind her that she was in her small kitchen apartment. She had an unusual obsession with roosters and her kitchen was decked out in cock-a-doodle-doos. "Where the hell are you? And why are you naked?"

"I have pants on." He pointed the camera down to show his bright red pants. "I'm trying to strap these pillows to my waist."

Her face scrunched up with even more confusion. "You're what?"

Dash held up his Santa hat to remind her.

Nell laughed, then took a bite of something off a large

spoon from her stove. "I forgot you were doing that. Lilian really wasn't kidding, was she?"

"Mom doesn't have a sense of humor, but she tries," Dash replied, finally getting the two pillows anchored to his stomach. He pulled the jacket overtop and attempted to button it up. "She's been asking if you're coming for Christmas Eve dinner, by the way."

"I know." Nell sighed and leaned down, propping herself up on her elbows in front of the camera. "I'm thinking about it."

"Come on, Nell. You know how much it would mean to her. Plus, none of us know what's going on with your life lately. You're like a vault." Dash pulled on the hat and adjusted his fake beard. He put out his hands in triumph. "There. Do I look like Saint Nick?"

Nell grinned and shook her head. "I'm going to need to come down to the mall sometime soon to watch you in action."

"You wouldn't dare," he threatened. "Gotta go, Nell. Christmas is calling."

She gave a quick wave and then disappeared from the screen. Dash grabbed his phone and tucked it into the waistband on his pants since he couldn't seem to find a pocket. Previous girlfriends had always complained about pants without pockets, but it wasn't until this moment that he realized how truly irritating that was.

Dash quickly tucked his previous clothes in an old grocery store bag and then left for the center of the mall. He was familiar with the Santa's Village set that was constructed in the mall's main hallway every winter, though he'd never actually participated in it before. Hell, he'd never done any sort of Santa or Christmas-themed activity until he'd moved in with the Winters. After they'd adopted him, he began to follow along with their Christmas traditions, of which there were many. The Winters did not play around when it came to holiday spirit. Their house was professional decorated, appropriately fake-snowed, and lit up bright enough to be seen the next county over.

"Santa!"

The moment Dash stepped out into the mall walkway, several little kids waved to him from behind ropes. His eyes widened as he tried to count how many children were in line, but he couldn't even see the end.

Dash waved to the crowd as a hefty, sweaty man wearing a too-tight elf costume came rushing toward him. "Uh, hello?"

"It's about time," the elf growled, grabbing the grocery bag from his hand and tossing it behind some fake presents. "Get up in your chair. Time is money, and Santa has a quota."

"He does?" Dash furrowed his brow. He was beginning to realize he should probably have asked more questions about the job to the other guy. "Oh, okay. I'll get started. What's your name?"

"Donner," the grumpy elf replied, speaking through a clenched smile that was clearly for show. "Now, let's go. I bring the kids to you, they tell you what they want. You promise them whatever they're asking for, hand them a little wrapped trinket, snap a picture for mom, and, lather, rinse, repeat."

Dash took his seat in the large red and gold throne, then waved a white-gloved hand at the line of children. Donner went to the front of the line and invited the first kid and her mother up to meet him in a sing-song voice that was clearly not his natural aggravated tone.

"Well, ho, ho, ho, young one," Dash greeted the little girl

as he helped her up onto his knee. "And what are you asking Santa for Christmas this year?"

"I want a unicorn. But it has to be rainbow." She began describing the intricate details of her unicorn dream and Dash just nodded along, chuckling. He promised her that he would see what he could do, and then they smiled for the formal photographer and for the mom who snapped a few cell phone pictures.

Next up was a slightly older boy, though he couldn't have been more than eight years old. Dash encouraged him to come on up, but the kid's feet were like concrete and he refused to move. His mother was pushing him forward, whispering harshly in his ear to *go*.

"Ho, ho, ho! Merry Christmas!" Dash greeted him once he was close enough.

The boy burst into tears and took off at a run. The mother apologized profusely and then went to chase after him.

"Rough start, Klaus." Donner shook his head and then turned a wide smile back to the crowd. "Next!"

An hour went by so fast, he hadn't even realized that he wasn't anywhere near the end of the line yet. In fact, it seemed like the line was just getting longer. Given that it was the middle of the day on a Saturday in early December, this wasn't exactly shocking.

It was, however, exhausting.

Dash enjoyed chatting with the kids about their Christmas wishes and he'd heard everything from wanting the latest Xbox to wanting parents reunited after a divorce. Despite his enjoyment, children were an incredible amount of energy. As a single man with no kids in his current life, he hadn't been fully prepared for both the volume and stickiness of this younger generation.

"Can I take a quick five?" Dash asked his elf helper between children. He glanced down at the wet candy cane stuck to his glove. "I just need to get some water. And maybe wash my hands."

Donner nodded and pulled the rope across the front of the line. "Santa's needed in his workshop! He'll be back in five minutes!"

There were a few groans from the families in line, but Dash tried not to feel guilty. He was technically only getting paid thirteen dollars an hour for this job, and he already needed a nap.

He'd move as quickly as possible, but there was no way in hell he was going back to that employee restroom by the dumpster.

Ignoring the awkward stares, Dash made his way—in full Santa gear—to the customer's bathroom off the main corridor. There was a short line of men waiting, but they were moving much quicker than the extensive line winding its way out of the ladies' room next door.

"Uh, you can go ahead of me, Santa," a young man stepped aside in line and offered him his spot.

He considered it for a moment, but he was in a rush. "Thanks, man."

"No problem. I don't want to be on your naughty list!" The young man was laughing now, and Dash rolled his eyes, but cut in front of him anyway.

After a quick visit to a stall, Dash found himself at the wide, multi-person sink trying to scrub off the candy cane now glued to his glove. A young boy came up to the sink next to him and began washing his hands, but his gaze was glued to Dash's reflection in the mirror before them.

Dash gave him a polite smile, then returned to his task.

The young boy pushed up on his tiptoes in order to turn

off the faucet. He paused and turned to face Dash. "Are you...are you Santa?"

He glanced down to see bright green eyes peeking out at him from under a thick mop of shaggy brown hair hanging low on the boy's forehead. "What?"

"Are you...um, are you Santa?"

Dash pulled his glove back on after he'd gotten off as much of the candy cane remnants off as possible. He smiled at the boy and deepened his voice. "I am. Merry Christmas!"

"My mom said we could come see you, but she's working all day," the young boy explained. "Can I tell you what I want for Christmas even though we're in a bathroom?"

Another man walked past them to the open sink, side-eying him. Dash cleared his throat and then got down on one knee. "Sure, kid. What's your name?"

"I'm Rudy." The boy beamed and straightened, standing taller. "Last year, you got me a model-making kit. I made a replica of the Eiffel Tower."

"That's pretty cool," Dash replied, chuckling and giving his best *ho ho ho* in the throaty laugh. "How'd it turn out?"

"Great! I love it! I still play with it," Rudy confessed. He was fidgeting with his hands now. "But, this year, can I ask for something for my mom?"

Dash tilted his head to the side. He smiled at the sweet concern on the boy's face. "Well, sure. Moms need Christmas gifts, too."

Rudy nodded. "I made her a picture with my teacher, too."

"Great job," Dash replied.

The boy stepped a little closer and lowered his voice slightly. "I was hoping you could teach my mom how to drive a sleigh."

He paused, considering the strange request. "You want me to teach your mom how to drive a sleigh?"

"She's *terrible* at driving," Rudy continued. "And she said that's why we don't have a car. But sleighs are harder to drive than cars, right? So, maybe if she learns how to drive a sleigh, then she can drive a car!"

"That is...well, that is some sound logic, son," Dash said with a laugh. "I can see this is important to you."

"It is," Rudy agreed. "I don't want to keep taking the bus everywhere. It's so smelly, and we have to get up so early to make it across town for her shift on weekends. I know she says it's fine, but I can tell she hates it, too."

Dash felt a thump in his chest as he pictured this little boy on a bus every weekend accompanying his mom to work. He certainly wasn't a stranger to buses. Hell, he'd spent most of his childhood using that as his sole means of transportation. Since finding the Winters, however, his life had changed dramatically. He had been gifted a car that he loved and refused to get rid of even years later when it had certainly seen better days. "Uh, so...where's your mom, kid?"

"I'll bring you to her!" Rudy grabbed his gloved hand and started pulling him toward the door. "Then you can tell her in person!"

Dash allowed himself to be led away, trying to figure out how he'd explain to Donner that he was teaching someone to drive a sleigh on his short bathroom break.

*Well, won't that be awkward.*

### Live on All Retailers:

https://booksbysarahrobinson.com/books/mall-i-want-for-christmas-is-you/

# EXCERPT FROM MALL YOU NEED IS LOVE

## A HOLIDAY ROMANCE

# CHAPTER ONE

## AMARA

*WHY AM I not even surprised?* Amara Hart scrunched up her nose as she stared at her ex-boyfriend's Tinder profile on her iPhone screen. She'd just been swiping to pass the time during her shift at work when she'd come across him, and now she found herself reading his bio with disgust.

*Aaron, 34: Looking for someone who can be discrete. DM for digits.*

She closed out of Tinder and opened Instagram, checking to make sure she hadn't completely lost her mind when she thought she'd seen he'd gotten married recently. Sure enough, when she got to his profile feed, there were tons of photos of him and a cute blonde wearing a giant engagement ring on their honeymoon. They'd literally gotten married last week, and he was already back on Tinder? Hell, it was Valentine's Day this weekend!

Once a cheater, always a cheater. Man, she'd really dodged that bullet.

Not that she really considered Aaron to be much of an outlier, though. After Aaron—and a slew of other short-term relationships that had all ended in heartbreak and disappointment—Amara had committed to staying single for the foreseeable future. Hell, maybe forever. Relationships were for people who were willing to settle for mediocre, and love was a Hallmark scam meant to pad the pockets of corporate bigwigs who preyed on lonely people on a commercialized holiday. Bah humbug, or whatever the Valentine's Day version of that was.

At thirty-two years old, Amara knew she still had a lot of life left to live, though she couldn't help but feel like the dating years were behind her. Good riddance.

"Frogger is on the fritz," Jean announced as she walked up to where Amara was standing, leaning against the cash-out counter. "Can you fix it again?"

The young teenager was leaving for college in the fall and Amara wasn't sure what she was going to do without her. When Amara had first opened Rad Retro Arcade three years ago on the west end of Yule Heights Shopping Mall, she hadn't expected her small town in Michigan to respond so well to a room full of original video game consoles and tables. She had everything from Pac-Man to Donkey Kong and she valued her little business as a place to step back in time and leave all her current woes at the door, and thanks to being pleasantly single, she didn't have any woes to worry about right now.

"Did you unplug it and then plug it back in?" Amara asked. That was always her first question, and half the time, it did solve the problem.

Jean rolled her big blue eyes. "Yes. Twice. I think you have to do a system reset."

"All right, all right," Amara agreed, heading over to find the Frogger machine by the SkeeBall ramps lining the back wall, currently packed with four different groups of teenagers all cheering one another on. She smiled at them, glad to see them here having fun with one another in person instead of on their cell phones ignoring the world from sepa- rate rooms. One of her regulars sank a high score ball, and she offered him a thumbs-up. "Good shot, Marco!"

"Thanks, Mara!" the young boy called back, using her nickname. "Hey, can we get some cheese fries?"

"Sure, kid." She had already asked the kitchen to prep an order when she'd seen them come in. Marco didn't often have enough money to play the games and order food, so usually he did one or the other. Sometimes she liked to make sure he was able to do both, so she'd send him some free fries from the restaurant down the hall. While she didn't have a kitchen of her own, she had worked out a part- nership with The Big Cheese food truck parked in the courtyard, along with eight other food trucks that served all the mall patrons. They provided her customers with a small discount on food, and she let them use her storage room after-hours for supplies.

After a few minutes of fiddling with the Frogger gaming system, she got it up and working again but had lost the last week of high scores data people had been accumulating. She frowned, hating when things like that happened, but thankful that it was only a week's worth. She glanced over at the Ms. Pac-Man game a few rows down, praying that never happened to her high score record there. In fact, she'd once been Michigan's highest scorer for the entire game and she'd been working on making a national title for herself before the championship league had been shut down for lack of funding...and interest.

Story of her life.

"It's working again," Mara told Jean as she returned to the counter. "Can you go check on the last two orders at The Big Cheese? They should be ready for pick up."

Jean nodded, then pointed toward the receiver for the landline against the wall. "Yeah, but you just missed a call from the charmer next door. Don't worry, I got him to call his dogs off."

Mara internally groaned. "Let me guess, he said the kids were being too loud and disturbing his fancy, rich customers?"

She laughed, nodding her head. "I mean, not in those exact words, but I think that sums it up pretty well."

"Go get the cheese fries." Amara ushered her off, chuckling. Complaints from the neighbors weren't entirely uncommon, especially when she'd first opened and had stolen half the mall's customer base, who now spent hours in her arcade instead of purchasing trinkets from other mall vendors. But these days, the complaints all seemed to be coming from one place—Kisses and Karats Jewelry. She didn't know the store owner well, except for the rumors circulating around the other shop owners at the mall that he was a ladies' man. In fact, the owner of Tequila Mockingbird on the south end swore he'd broken her heart when he didn't returned her text messages after a date. One of the hairdressers at Barber Streisand said he saw him making out in the parking lot with the wife of the owner of Son of a Bun Bakery. All that to say, she had no interest in getting to know the reckless Casanova, nor was she interested in keeping her store quieter so that he could sell more diamonds to misguided saps who had too much money and not enough imagination.

Her luck was short-lasting as the entire arcade suddenly went dark.

"What the hell?" Amara stood up straighter, trying to adjust her eyes to the sudden blackout.

"Hey, what's going on? The game turned off!" A kid

"Hey, what's going on? The game turned off!" A kid from one end of the arcade complained loudly.

"Sorry, folks. The power will be back on in a minute," Amara announced, quickly making her way to the back room to find the circuit breaker. The rest of the mall still looked completely illuminated; only her store had gone off. What the heck was happening? She'd never had an outage in here before.

When she arrived at the circuit breaker, it took all her might to pry the metal panel apart, and when it released, it flew open so hard that it hit the wall behind it with a clang. She had never had to look in here before, and none of the switches in front of her were labeled as to where they went as she held her cell phone's flashlight up to the box. She examined it for a few seconds before deciding to just flip all of them and hope for the best.

Thankfully, that seemed to do the trick.

The back room lit up with the familiar fluorescent glare, and Amara sighed at the stack of video games that had toppled over against one wall. She went to pile them back up, not even sure why they'd been left here in the first place, when she real- ized the back door was ajar. Every store in the mall was connected by a small, dingy corridor that ran the length of the mall and allowed store owners to take out trash or receive shipments without walking it past the customers through the front door. Aside from the nightly trash run, she always kept the door locked, because the retro games she carried at her arcade were expensive, and she wasn't willing to see one of them walk off and end up on eBay for a collector to snatch up.

Amara pulled the door firmly closed, ensuring the bolt settled into place. She turned the lock, frowning as she made a mental note to remind Jean to be more careful when coming and going. As she returned to the floor, she passed out extra tokens as a courtesy to the customers who'd lost their gaming streaks with the outage, and everyone was appeased and happily playing again within minutes.

Jean walked in with a large tray full of cheese fries and other cheesy items. "Who ordered these again?"

Amara handed her the order slip with the names and locations of the customers. "Hey, did you leave the back door open earlier? All the power went out in here."

"Really?" Jean's brows lifted. "No, I haven't used the back door today."

"It was definitely weird, but I was able to get it back on pretty quickly," she confirmed. "But yeah, just make sure you keep that door locked."

The rest of the shift went by with no incident until Jean was putting on her jacket and getting ready to clock out. "Uh...Amara?"

"What?" She turned to look at the young girl, then followed her gaze to the three police officers walking through the front entrance of the arcade. "Uh oh."

"Should I stay?" Jean asked.

"Did you commit a crime?" Amara joked. "No, go on home. I'll talk to them. I'm sure it's just a complaint from *Kisses and Karats* again."

Jean rolled her eyes and gave a small chuckle before clocking out on the payroll app on her phone and then waving goodbye.

"Can I help you folks?" Amara asked as the police officers reached the counter where she was standing.

A tall man with a thick mustache tipped his hat to her. "Ma'am, we're here about the incident next door."

"Okay, we told him that we'd try to be quieter, but we can't control our customers. They're not being rambunctious or disorderly or anything. They are just playing." Amara waved her hand toward the room, indicating her gaming customers. "He didn't need to call the police on us."

A female officer standing to the mustachioed man's right frowned. "No, ma'am. This is about the robbery earlier today. We need to ask you a few questions."

*What?* "Wait...there was a robbery?" Amara's mind immediately went to the open back door, and she quickly scanned the arcade, trying to see if she could spot anything missing. Her stomach sank at the idea of having to make a report to insurance. Her rates were already insanely high, and this was just going to skyrocket them. "What was taken?"

"Not here, ma'am," the woman continued. "Next door. Over fifty thousand dollars' worth of jewelry was stolen from the back room at Kisses and Karats earlier today. Were you not aware of that?"

Her eyes went wide. "No! That's terrible. Is everyone okay?"

Despite her feelings toward her obstinate neighbor, she would never wish something like that on any small business owner.

The officer pulled out a notepad and a pen. "No one was injured, but we'd like to see any security footage you have from today, as well as anything suspicious you might have witnessed."

"Oh, uhm...I don't actually have any security cameras in here. The mall does in the main hallways, so, you know, I figured why double up on that expense?" Heat rose to her face, and she wondered if her explanation sounded as stupid out loud as it did in her head. In trying to minimize her monthly expenses, that hadn't seemed like the most important thing to focus on, but now she was second-guessing that decision. "I did find the back door unlocked earlier, though. That was strange. It's never unlocked or left open, and my employee said she hadn't used it all day. Nothing was missing from our back room." She frowned. "I guess I *could* double check more thoroughly."

"Why don't you go do that," the officer agreed. "Officer Powell will come with you and we'll take a look around, if that's okay."

"Sure, help yourself." She gestured to the store floor. "Just don't try to beat my Ms. Pac Man record."

Her joke fell flat as the hairy-lipped officer frowned at her. "We're working, ma'am."

"Right, uh...okay, well, this way." Amara headed toward the back room as the female police officer followed close behind. The room was pretty small, and not exactly the picture of organization, but it was pretty easy to see that everything that was supposed to be there was there. "Nothing seems to be missing."

"What happened there?" Officer Powell pointed to the circuit breaker that she'd left open to remind herself to test each switch later and label them.

"Oh, the power went off earlier. I guess the fuse box blew, but I flipped the switches, and it came back on pretty quickly. I just need to label them, because that's never happened before."

"The power went off?" The officer's brows raised, and she pulled out her notepad and a pen. "What time was this?" Of course, that was something that they would have wanted to know about. She couldn't believe she hadn't already mentioned that. "Uh, around one o'clock, I guess?

Lunch time, for sure. But it was very quick."

"I'm going to need you to write a statement about all of

this." Officer Powell handed her a form. "Do you have a pen, or do you need one?"

"I have one," Amara said, grabbing one off the back table. "Uh, sure. I'll just fill this out now."

The officer stood stoically and watched as she began writing.

She didn't have much to say, but she repeated the information she'd given the officers and then included her contact information before handing the form back to her. "Here you go."

"The store owner next door would like to talk with you as well," the officer commented as they headed out of the back office.

*Great.* She secretly groaned but gave a tight-lipped smile. "Sure thing."

Dealing with the Hallmark playboy was the last thing she wanted to do today.

## Live on All Retailers:

https://booksbysarahrobinson.com/books/mall-you-need-is-love/

# EXCERPT FROM MALL OUT OF LUCK

A HOLIDAY ROMANCE

# CHAPTER ONE

## NELL

*Did you see this?*

Nell James read the text message that popped up on her phone followed by a link to a local blog article. Her best friend, Mara Hart, spent way too much time on social media and was always the first one to send her breaking news—or post cute Instagram pictures of her and her husband Val doing cute, romantic things around town. Not that Nell wasn't happy for her—she was—but with Valentine's Day only a few weeks behind her, it had become painfully obvious how single she still was.

She pulled the impact goggles off her face and placed them next to the beaker she'd just been working with before scanning the article attached to the link.

**Throwback Jack's Under New Ownership—Launch on March 17, 2022.**

*What!* Nell texted Mara back immediately upon seeing the title. *TJ closed?*

She'd been going to Throwback Jack's for over five years now and was part of a local darts league that always practiced there. Being a vaccine scientist during the day meant that she needed time to unwind in the evening and on weekends, and playing darts with other thirty-year-olds in a recreational league had been a big source of that for her lately. Her current efforts at her job on the Sandfly Fever Sicilian Virus vaccine project were at a standstill, and she'd been going out after work more often than ever before.

Not that she was about to advertise that to her colleagues or invite them to join her.

Being a woman in the field of STEM (Science, Technology, Engineering, and Mathematics) was hard enough, but being a former-foster-child, current-lesbian in STEM? The misogyny deck had been stacked against her from day one. She'd had to prove herself twice as competent as the men on her team just to earn the same level of respect—and even that still meant she'd get the occasional ask to *be a doll and grab me a coffee, won't you?*

Ugh. The reminder made her stomach lurch with patriarchal resentment. She made a mental note to call her adopted brother, Dash—also a former-foster kid—and tell him about the latest office antics with Mr. Staffi down the hall from her where he'd formally written human resources to complain about free tampons in the women's room and nothing free in the men's room. Dash lived on the other side of the country with his little, happy family now, but he still knew how to throw in a well-timed joke that made her feel better when she was feeling ragey towards "the man."

Despite those obstacles in her career path, she'd managed to work her way up to one of the top positions in her organization and was a leading researcher on this current vaccine project. Simply put, she was proud of all she'd accomplished.

*No, they're open now.* Mara responded to her previous text message. *The soft start was yesterday, I guess. Big launch on St. Patty's Day. We should go! I bet Val can close the store for a day or get someone to cover. You can be our third wheel!*

Nell frowned but felt a little relief that at least the bar was still open—only to have that quickly disappear at the thought of being yet another third wheel to her friend's happy love story. She wondered why she hadn't heard anything from the darts league, and if that meant that things were changing for the upcoming Pot O' Gold St. Patrick's Day tournament that Throwback Jack's used to host every year.

*Maybe I should go tonight and find out?* She clicked back onto the link and read the article further.

**It's no secret that Throwback Jack's has been struggling over the last few years to appeal to a younger audience, so when news came that ownership had changed, no one here at Michigan Mishigas was surprised. But when we learned who the new owner was though? Things became interesting, to say the least.**

**Saoirse (pronounced Sur-Sha) Walsh hails from a town of less than five hundred people in Nebraska—and she's already left three of them at the altar. Now she's come to Yule Heights, Michigan with plans to launch a bar named The Lucky Leprechaun right where Throwback Jack's used to be. This writer thinks The Unlucky Leprechaun might be a better fitting name at this point!**

She chuckled lightly at the blogger's commentary, though she couldn't imagine the focal point of the piece would feel the same way if she read it. She clicked the photograph included with the article and pulled up a picture of a woman with bright red hair and dark green eyes —almost emerald—standing behind a bar with a big smile on her face that looked like she was ready to take on the world. Too bad there was a cut-out photo in the bottom right that was three different engagement photo shoots—all different partners with Saoirse, including two men and one woman, all obscured to hide the almost-spouses faces for (she assumed) privacy reasons. The caption under the photo read: "I almost do!"

*Man, they're really taking this poor girl's back story and running with it.*

Nell opened up her text messages to Mara again and sent back a quick laughing face emoji. *Oh my God, the byline though.*

*Right? They don't have high hopes for that place,* Mara responded seconds later.

*She's hot though,* Nell replied.

She clicked over to the woman's photo again, examining her a moment longer. She really was beautiful, and there was something freeing about already knowing Saoirse was interested in women before having even met her. It wasn't that Yule Heights was super conservative, but it was very small. There were maybe four lesbians who lived in this town that were open and out, and maybe twice that number of gay men. If she wanted a date, she had to set her Tinder settings to pretty far out because she'd learned quickly that mucking around in her own town was a recipe for disaster. And she wasn't just saying that because the last woman she dated was a chef at the only fancy restaurant in town and now that place was off limits to her for the rest of time. She already missed their garlic bread.

"Nell?" Mr. Staffi popped his head in her laboratory

door. His nose wrinkled and he squinted his eyes at her. "Is that smell coming from in here?"

She frowned and sniffed the air. Nothing was striking her as out of the ordinary, and she glanced at the chemicals she was working with—all of which were odorless. "No, not me."

"You know, you *could* bring in some deodorizer." Mr. Staffi lifted his nose in the air just enough to be looking down at her—his favorite way of viewing the world. "We don't provide it, but most scientists bring their own if they know they're going to be working with such pungent smells."

Nell cleared her throat and walked over to the doorway where he was standing. In a loud, exaggerated sound, she sniffed the air. "I don't know, Mr. Staffi. That doesn't smell like my aluminum hydroxide. It *does*, however, smell like...did you have tuna for lunch, Mr. Staffi?"

His face tinged a darker shade of his normal red. "Well, yes. I did. But that was yesterday."

"I think that's it." She pushed back on her heels and crossed her arms over her chest. "You've got the tuna mouth."

So dark red, his face was nearly purple. "I will have you know that I brush my teeth every night and morning."

"But did you scrape your tongue?" She used a light-hearted lilt in her voice now, enjoying that she was driving him nuts. Served him right. Dealing with him day in and day out in the office next door was exhausting. "That's what people always forget. The smell is stuck to your tongue. It's the Tuna Tongue. And I'm so sorry to say, but it's not curable."

His nostrils flared and he rolled his eyes. "I'm reporting

this to Human Resources." He turned on his heels and stomped down the hallway. "This office smells."

Nell stuck her head out the door, watching him walk away and unable to resist one final quip. "Ask for Susie. She has my number on speed dial!"

She laughed as she walked back into her office and glanced at the clock. It was already well into the evening hours, and she would have been off hours ago if she hadn't become wrapped up in this project she was working on. *Oh, well.* Now seemed like as good a time as any to call it quits for the day and maybe give this new bar a try on her way home.

And maybe meet a new woman...

## Live on All Retailers:

https://booksbysarahrobinson.com/books/mall-out-of-luck/

# EXCERPT FROM MALL AMERICAN GIRL

A HOLIDAY ROMANCE

# CHAPTER ONE

## KAMAR

"A HOT DOG EATING CONTEST?" Kamar Jaziri frowned as he tried to absorb everything his boss was telling him.

Harold, an older man with thick glasses, shrugged as if he hadn't just tried to strong-arm Kamar into an event he wanted nothing to do with. "Not just hot dogs. There's also the potato sack race and the dunk tank."

Harold was the operations manager at Yule Heights Shopping Mall, and he'd hired Kamar for the summer to play for the evening crowds on Thursday and Friday nights. While the gig wasn't particularly well paid, it was over a holiday weekend, and the July Fourth crowd tended to tip nicely. Also thankfully, the pavilion where he'd be performing from was set right outside the entrance to The Lucky Leprechaun, the mall's only bar, so Kamar was hoping some drunk patrons might find their way out and be even more generous with their tips.

But nowhere in his job description had it said anything about potatoes and hot dogs.

He blinked slowly. "And I have to do this *why?*"

"Hey, the majority of this job is the tips." Harold

pointed toward the small stage set up in the center pavilion of the Yule Heights Shopping Mall. "We pay jack shit to our musicians—not my fault, I always try to advocate for more, but the higher-ups run the show. You're going to have to hustle if you want to rake in actual money here, and that means being part of the Yule Heights Independence Games and bumping elbows with vendors who can funnel people your way. How many hot dogs can you eat in a minute?"

Kamar wanted to laugh, but he wasn't sure if his new boss had the same sense of humor he did. Was he seriously asking him that question? Or was everyone in this town really into these Independence Games like he said? Being from out of state until recently moving here for college, these weren't exactly the type of festivities he was used to, growing up in New York City. Heck, he couldn't remember the last time he'd even seen a real New Yorker eat a hot dog —that was reserved for tourists and people with iron stomachs.

"Uh, I'm not sure. So, I just need to eat some hot dogs, run a race, and that's it?" he asked.

Harold nodded, but then his eyes lit up. "And you have to shoot the deer!"

"Absolutely not." The words came out of Kamar's mouth before he had a chance to try to censor himself. He cringed at the thought of hurting an animal. He was a gentle soul—as his music taste and style made very clear—and murdering Bambi just wasn't on his summer reading list. "Are you telling me that there is hunting involved in this, too?"

Harold laughed—a loud guffaw that tipped his entire head back and made his belly shake. "I hear you loud and clear there, son, but no. That game just involves shooting the fake deer with a soft water pistol to keep them away from your flowers. No real deer involved. You know, my brother was a musician back in the day—rest his soul. Wouldn't hurt a fly, but man would he go to town beating the hell out of some drums."

Kamar grinned at that, though his instrument of choice was acoustic guitar most of the time. He could also play bass and some keyboard, but when he was on stage singing ballads, the acoustic guitar felt the most authentic to him and the message he wanted to portray to the crowd. "Sounds like my kind of guy."

"Your folks live around here?" Harold asked.

Kamar shook his head. "My father's home in New York. He's probably asleep by now—usually snoring by seven on the dot."

"Good man." Harold tipped his chin, nodding his approval. He glanced at his watch, pushing his glasses back up his nose as they slid down. "My Ruth and I are usually the same way. Hence the reason I'm going to head out now so I can get home to her. Let me know if you need anything, but everything should be there."

He pointed one last time toward the pavilion then turned and headed down the main corridor of the mall toward the manager's office at the other end. Kamar looked around him, taking in the different stores facing his small stage—an eyeglasses store called Eye Carumba, Kwik Ink Printing, Summer's Sun Tanning Salon, and the Twisted Bread Pretzel Shop were the closest to him. Somewhere nearby must be a candle store as well, because the scent of flowers and wax was strong in the air.

Certainly not his ideal stage for playing music, but he'd played in worse. And a Master's Degree in music education was not cheap. With the fall semester's tuition already looming heavily on his bank account, he was more than willing to make ends meet however he could.

Kamar got to work on setting up his equipment. There wasn't too much to do except place his combo amplifier next to his microphone stand. He started first with pinning the small banner he'd had printed years ago that he used at all his shows, despite the fact that the ink was beginning to fade. He'd had to pay a premium for each color he wanted to use, so he'd scrapped his original idea entirely. It was now just a simple black banner with white letters reading MUSIC LIKE THE MOON and then his contact information below, including a way to tip him directly via Venmo or CashApp.

He tended toward softer ballads and soul-filled songs that he'd written himself, and when he'd combined that with the original meaning of his name in Arabic, it had just seemed right to brand his music under that name. When his mother Djamila had still been living, she'd regularly complimented his crooning voice and told him that she'd named him after the moon because he was destined to be among the stars.

These days, though, he was beginning to feel less and less like stardom was in his journey.

When the stage was finally aesthetically to his liking, Kamar began plugging in the amp and microphone stand into the outlet on the floor covered by a small, removable grate. He clicked on the amp as soon it was plugged in, but nothing happened. Kamar frowned, then tapped the microphone. Still nothing. Returning to the outlet, he took everything out of the plugs and then put them back in.

Zero power.

Kamar felt his stomach tighten as anxiety swelled in his gut. Thankfully, he had Harold's phone number in his cell so he called him to figure out a solution. But the phone just kept ringing until it went to a message that stated Harold's voicemail was full. Then the line went dead.

"Hey, any chance you know how to get this outlet turned on?" Kamar asked a man walking past the stage who was in maintenance coveralls pushing a mop bucket.

The man removed the headphones in his ears long enough to hear the question, but then put them back in, shrugged his shoulders, and continued walking on.

Kamar surveyed what was around him, but his options were either wait for Harold to answer the phone and miss out on any potential tips in the meantime—or find someone to lend him power.

The bar was not an option since he was worried about drunk patrons tripping over extension cords and suing the pants off him. The pretzel stand next door was completely dark and had a metal gate pulled closed in front of it. The third option was Summer's Sun, a tanning salon that was brighter than any other storefront in the mall.

*Bingo!*

Unwilling to leave his guitar case unattended, Kamar took it with him as he walked over to the tanning salon. The moment he stepped onto the black-and-white checkered tile floor of the salon, a woman sitting behind the receptionist counter looked up at him with interest.

"Hi, are you the owner?" Kamar placed his hand out between them to introduce himself.

She stood from the chair she'd been sitting in and placed the magazine in her hands on the counter before reaching forward and accepting his hand. "I am. Summer Darby. Are you looking for a tanning service? We also sell packages, if you're considering purchasing for a friend or girlfriend."

He smiled, appreciating that she was going right into sales mode. Clearly, she was a hustler like he was if she owned her own place like this. "Actually, I was wondering if I could ask a favor. One mall vendor to another."

Summer lifted a brow as she waited for him to continue.

"I'm playing out on the pavilion there and need power for my amp. The outlet isn't working, but I have a long extension cord and was hoping to hook it up to your outlet here." He pointed at the outlet by the front door that currently had only one of the two sockets taken. "It'll just be for a few hours and that's it."

She frowned. "I don't know...I pay the electric bill here and it isn't cheap. How many watts is the amp?"

"Ten," he replied. "But I don't want to put you out. What if I hang up a sign by my stand telling people to come in here? You could consider it a marketing expense."

Summer seemed a bit more appeased at that idea. "I guess that could make sense if it actually does bring people in."

She didn't seem fully convinced yet.

"Has it been busy today?" he asked, placing his guitar case on the floor by his feet and leaning against the counter. "I've never actually been in a tanning booth before."

"Spray tan," she corrected and then shook her head. "Well, it's not for everyone. Myself included, of course. I'm as pale as a sheet of paper."

Summer gestured toward her own skin, but Kamar found his gaze traveling down her entire frame slowly. She wasn't the smallest woman, and yet every curve was in the right place. Her clothes were snug, but in a purposeful way, and her shirt cut down just low enough in the front to make him pause there for a second.

"You don't use your own product?" Kamar asked, his

gaze returning to her eyes as he felt his cheeks heat, upon realizing he'd just blatantly checked her out. Hopefully she hadn't noticed. That wasn't even his usual behavior since he certainly wasn't interested in romances right now as he was trying to get through graduate school. Something about the way this woman held herself, though...it was intriguing. "Why do you run a tanning salon then?"

"Even if I don't use it often, I'm pretty passionate about giving women an easy and affordable alternative to tanning that is safe for their skin and their health," Summer replied, sitting back down in the chair behind her. "Not enough people take skin cancer and sun safety seriously."

Her last few words sounded strained, and he wanted to ask her more, but it didn't feel like it was his place. Plus, he really did need the power turned on so he could get started earning tips.

"Oh," he replied simply, unsure what else to say. "I hear it'll be pretty sunny this weekend at the Yule Heights Independence Games."

*Out of everything in the world, how was that the only thing he could think to say?*

But her chin lifted, and her brows were raised when she took in his face. "You're competing in that?"

"Didn't seem to have much of a choice not to," he said with a dry laugh. "Harold seemed pretty insistent."

Her face softened and she smiled. "Harold's a good guy. Old school, but a romantic." She looked at him carefully for another moment, studying his face as if she was looking for something. What that was, he wasn't sure.

Finally, she gestured toward the outlet he'd seen earlier. "The plug is over there. You just need to make sure to tape down the wire so people don't trip over it."

He pushed up to a standing position. "Thank you. I really appreciate it."

"Good luck," she called out to him while he began setting up the extension cord. "I mean, tomorrow at the games."

Kamar grinned. "Are you in it, too?"

"How can I not?" Her smile flattened more into a smug grin, and she wiggled her brows. "After all, I'm the undefeated champion for the last four years running. Wouldn't want anything to change that now."

He stopped in his tracks, turning back to look at her. "You're the undefeated champion...in the hot dog eating contest?"

"If your mind is going somewhere dirty, then you can take a hike," she replied, pointing out into the mall.

Kamar shook his head—*that* thought hadn't crossed his mind. Well, not until right this moment. Jesus, now that mental image was front and center. "No, no, I mean...how many hot dogs did you eat to win last year?"

"It's a sixty second timer, and last year I won with twelve hot dogs." The way she said it so casually was like this was an everyday occurrence. "The year before that, I did eleven."

"In sixty seconds?" he asked again, an incredulous tone seeping into his voice. His gaze swept over her frame again —*where the heck was she putting those hot dogs?* "There's zero chance that's real. Six-zero seconds? Like one single minute?"

"I'll have you know that the world record for ten minutes is seventy-six hot dogs, so it's absolutely possible." Her hands were on her hips now, her chin tilted up just enough so that she could look down her nose at him. "Tomorrow, my goal is thirteen."

He grinned at her. "Well, well, well...never thought I'd say this, but you're going to have some competition this year. I'm going to eat you out."

"What?" Her eyes widened.

"I mean in hot dogs. Like, I'm going to out-eat you. I'm going to eat more hot dogs than you. In the contest." He was stumbling over his words now. *Why the hell had he suddenly lost any semblance of chill around this woman?* "Like as a competitor, in uh, in business. Uh, um, well, I'm going to go start my set. See you tomorrow!"

With that, he turned on his heel and practically ran out of the tanning salon and straight for the pavilion. Flirting, dating...any sort of romantic whim was off the table right now, and he couldn't believe he'd said something so potentially suggestive. That was not like him—his style was romance, not crudeness. Plus, he wasn't in a place in his life where he'd even be able to give attention to a partner—he had to focus on school and earning money for his life post-graduate degree.

That had to be enough for now.

*Focus,* he reminded himself as he confirmed that the outlet was finally working and he had the power he needed.

Kamar stepped onto the pavilion stage, the guitar against his chest, and breathed the first few words of his song into the microphone...

*Under the moonlit palm tree, there was a boy who dreamt of the sun...*

## Live on All Retailers:

https://booksbysarahrobinson.com/books/mall-american-girl/

# ABOUT THE AUTHOR

*Contemporary Romances Across the Rainbow*

Sarah Robinson first started her writing career as a published poet in high school, and then continued in college, winning several poetry awards and being published in multiple local literary journals.

Never expecting to make a career of it, a freelance writing Craigslist job accidentally introduced her to the world of book publishing. Lengthening her writing from poetry to novels, Robinson published her first book through a small press publisher, before moving into self-publishing, and then finally accepting a contract from Penguin Random House two years later. She continues to publish both traditionally and indie with over 18+ novels to her name with publishers like Penguin, Waterhouse Press, Hachette, and more. She has achieved awards and accolades including 2021 Vivian Award Finalist, Top 10 iBooks Bestseller, Top 25 Amazon Kindle Bestseller, and Top 5 Barnes & Noble Bestseller. She has been published in three languages.

In her personal life, Sarah Robinson is happily married to the gentle giant of her dreams with one rambunctious toddler and another baby on the way. They have a home full of love, snuggly pets, and are happily living in Arlington, Virginia.

Did You Enjoy This Novella? Leave a Review!

You can help the author by **leaving a review**! Reviews on the online book retailer where you purchased this novella help the author so much!

I Want To Do More! How Else Can I Help?

If you want to get even more involved and help the author, you can follow Sarah on social media and interact online! You can join Sarah's Facebook Reader Group (Robinson's Ramblings) and/or her newsletter! You can also follow any of her social media sites below!

Follow the Author on Social Media

booksbysarahrobinson.com
subscribepage.com/sarahrobinsonnewsletter
facebook.com/booksbysarahrobinson

twitter.com/booksby_sarah
goodreads.com/booksbysarahrobinson
instagram.com/booksbysarahrobinson

BARE

SHEER

## At the Mall Series

*(Romantic Comedy Shorts)*

Mall I Want for Christmas is You

Mall You Need is Love

Mall Out of Luck

Mall American Girl

Mall-O-Ween Mischief

Mall Year Long: The Box Set

## Heart Lake Series

*(Small Town Romances)*

Dreaming of a Heart Lake Christmas

The Little Bookstore on Heart Lake Lane (Coming May 2023)

*More coming...*

## Queer Romantic Comedies *(coming soon!)*

Baby Bank

Les-Be-Honest

Dopplebanger

## Standalone Novels

Not a Hero: A Bad Boy Marine Romance

Misadventures in the Cage

One Night Stand Serial

Second Shot of Whiskey

**Women's Fiction**

Every Last Drop

More books and series by Sarah Robinson are coming soon, check her website for the latest news and releases, or subscribe to her newsletter to never miss one!